HARRY

VERSUS

THE FIRST 100 DAYS OF SCHOOL

ALSO BY EMILY JENKINS

Middle-Grade

Toys Go Out

Toy Dance Party

Toys Come Home

Younger Readers

All-of-a-Kind Family Hanukkah

A Greyhound, A Groundhog

Toys Meet Snow

A Fine Dessert: Four Centuries, Four Families, One Delicious Treat

Lemonade in Winter

ALSO ILLUSTRATED BY PETE OSWALD

The Sad Little Fact

HARRY
VERSUS
THE FIRST 100 DAYS OF SCHOOL

by
EMILY JENKINS
pictures by
PETE OSWALD

a·s·b
anne schwartz books

In memory of Lillian Meckler —E.J.

For my first-grade teacher, Mrs. Acosta —P.O.

Text copyright © 2021 by Emily Jenkins
Jacket art and illustrations copyright © 2021 by Pete Oswald

Visit us on the Web! rhcbooks.com

Educators and librarians, for a variety of teaching tools, visit us at RHTeachersLibrarians.com

Library of Congress Cataloging-in-Publication Data
Names: Jenkins, Emily, author. | Oswald, Pete, illustrator.
Title: Harry versus the first 100 days of school / Emily Jenkins;
illustrated by Pete Oswald.
Other titles: Harry vs. the first 100 days of school
Description: First edition. | New York: Anne Schwartz Books, [2021] |
Audience: Ages 5–8. | Audience: Grades K–3. | Summary: Harry Bergen-Murphy does not feel ready when he starts first grade, but by day 100 he has become an expert on several important things, including being a first-grader.
Identifiers: LCCN 2019028297 | ISBN 978-0-525-64471-2 (hardcover) | ISBN 978-0-525-64472-9 (library binding) | ISBN 978-0-525-64473-6 (ebook)
Subjects: CYAC: Schools—Fiction. | Friendship—Fiction. | Family life—Fiction.
First day of school—Fiction. | Hundredth day of school—Fiction.
Classification: LCC PZ7.J4134 Har 2020 | DDC [E]—dc23

The text of this book is set in 13-point Century Schoolbook.
The illustrations were rendered digitally with scanned watercolor textures.
Book design by Rachael Cole

MANUFACTURED IN SINGAPORE
1 3 5 7 9 10 8 6 4 2
First Edition

CONTENTS

Prologue
HOME

Harry Bergen-Murphy has a pack of ten yellow pencils.

He has last year's water bottle.

He has a new Fluff Monster lunchbox and new green sneakers.

First grade starts tomorrow! Harry will go to the Graham School, also known as Public School 48, in Brooklyn, New York. His teacher will be Ms. Peek-Schnitzel.

A too-short haircut: yeah, that happened. When he looks in the mirror, all he can see are his giant ears. He will be the eariest kid in first grade, probably. He rubs his hand over his hair. It feels tickly.

Harry is stuck using his old backpack for first grade. It's brown and kind of ugly. But there *is* a new Fluff

1

Monster key chain hanging off the zipper. His sister, Charlotte, gave it to him. It's his favorite monster: Gar-Gar, the black-and-yellow one that looks like a bumble bee.

Fluff Monsters are the silliest monsters in the world. Harry loves them. They are characters in a video game. They go *whomple whomple* when they run. Harry plays the game on his mom's tablet.

"Are you ready for the first day of school?" says Mommy, tucking Harry into bed. She strokes his hair. "You'll be a great first grader."

Harry pushes out his lower lip. He is not sure she is right, but he doesn't know how to say it.

"Are you worried?" she asks.

Harry nods.

"I can understand that. But I know you, H," she says. "I *know* you are ready."

Still, Harry lies awake for a long time after she hugs him goodnight.

He worries about getting lost in the big school building. About strict teachers. And rules. And learning to read. Mean kids and scary classroom guinea pigs.

He doesn't feel ready at all.

Chapter 1
DON'T LEAVE ME

DAY 1. WEDNESDAY, SEPTEMBER 5

Harry *has* been to day care before. He went to kindergarten, too, but that was in the trailers on the other side of the play yard. First-grade classrooms are in the big-kid school.

The Graham School is four blocks from home. Harry walks with his sister, Charlotte. Mommy is a little ways behind. "If you need me," says Charlotte, "I'll be upstairs in fourth grade, room three-oh-three. Plus we have lunch and recess at the same time, so you'll see me then. Got it?"

Harry nods. The weather still feels like summer. The trees on their street are bright green. Charlotte wears red shorts and a new T-shirt with sequins, plus her favorite running shoes. She has two braids in her hair. Harry is wearing his green sneakers, blue shorts, and his favorite shirt with four horses.

"Will there be guinea pigs at school?" he asks.

"Don't worry about guinea pigs, H. Really."

"What if kids are mean?"

"Some people are mean, yeah," says Charlotte. "But boo on them. Just don't hang out with them."

Harry stops walking. "Will the teachers yell?"

"The music teacher yells. But I still like her. She plays the accordion."

Yelling? No way. Harry turns and starts to run back home. He zooms past Mommy, down the block. He climbs the steps to his apartment building and plasters his body against the front door. "I'm not going to school!"

His mom follows. "H, what's wrong?"

"There are mean kids and yelling teachers! Charlotte said so!"

"Did not," says Charlotte, catching up. "I was just being realistic."

"I'm not going!"

His mother pats his back. "H," she says, bending over. "What are you scared of?"

Harry wants to say, "I might not make friends! What if someone picks on me? What if I get in trouble? What if I'm the only one who can't read yet?" He wants to say all that, but it won't come out. Instead, he says, "You can't make me go!"

Mommy holds out her hand. "School is fun," she says kindly. "You'll make so many friends, and you'll learn like, one hundred things every day."

"No!"

"How about we look in your lunch bag," she says. "See? I packed your favorites."

She holds it open and Harry peeks in. Cucumber, cantaloupe, pork dumplings, and strawberry yogurt in a squeezy tube. At the bottom of the bag are two square butter cookies wrapped in wax paper.

Those *are* his favorites. Especially the cookies. Harry doesn't usually get dessert at lunchtime. "That's a good lunch in there," he admits.

Mommy holds out her hand again. It is her nice Mommy hand, with shiny blue fingernails she paints herself.

Harry sniffs back his tears and grabs on.

"I think you are ready," Mommy says. "I really, truly do."

He lets her walk him to school.

They all three climb the steps that lead to a fat brick

building with a spiky black fence. Mommy has to say goodbye at the door.

Harry hugs her. Then he takes a deep breath and he does it.

With Charlotte right beside him, Harry Bergen-Murphy goes to school.

DAY 2. THURSDAY, SEPTEMBER 6

School was all right yesterday.

The first-grade classroom is full of markers and pattern blocks. There is not a single guinea pig anywhere. Ms. Peek-Schnitzel, the teacher, has a bright voice and a face like an apple, shiny and pink. She is old and wears makeup on her eyebrows. She said hello to the kids as they entered and assigned each one a seat at a table. The tables are labeled with animal names: Goat, Sheep, Rabbit, Cow, and Horse.

Harry is at Goat Table. It has a laminated picture of a goat on it.

Some sections of the classroom wall are covered with corkboard. And others with whiteboard. Plus there is a SMART Board near the teacher's special chair. Lots of boards! In one corner is a reading area with a shaggy carpet and bins full of picture books. In another is a large rug with colored squares. Each student gets a square to sit on during morning meeting. Harry's spot is on a green square. And green is his favorite color!

Ms. Yoo, the art teacher, visited after lunch. She is a round person with streaks of pink in her hair and lots of rings on her fingers. She handed out watercolor paints and invited all the kids to make self-portraits.

Harry already knew kids from kindergarten: Mason and Mia, Adam and Abigail. Harry likes Mason a whole lot. His ears stick out almost as much as Harry's. He was wearing a shirt with a pineapple on it. The two of them played at recess. The big-kid yard doesn't have grass like the kindergarten yard, but it does have climbing structures and rubber matting. Mason and Harry went to the top of the tall structure everyone calls the Rocket.

Some things were still hard. When they played a

Name Game, using their fingers, Harry messed up when it was his turn.

Harry Harry Harry
Whoops! Harry
Whoops! Harry
Harry Harry

He forgot the second *Whoops!* and felt his face heat up. Then he looked at the carpet for the rest of the game.

Now he and Charlotte walk upstairs for the second day of school. "Bye," says Charlotte, outside his classroom. "Have a good day, H."

Ms. Peek-Schnitzel's door is covered with bright paper polka dots. Each dot has a kid's name on it: Harry, Mason, and twenty-three others. There are twenty-five kids in all.

Suddenly, they seem like stranger polka dots.

"Don't leave me!" cries Harry. He starts to cry. He can't help it.

"You have to be a big Harry when you're in first grade," says Charlotte.

"Don't leave me with the polka dots!" cries Harry.

Charlotte gives him a hug. "I have no idea what you're talking about," she says into his ear. "I can't be late, 'kay? Bye!" She pulls away and heads upstairs.

"You're a guinea pig!" Harry yells.

Ms. Peek-Schnitzel leans into the hall. "Harry, my friend, is that you?" she says.

"Yes."

"Do you know how to work an electric pencil sharpener?"

Harry does.

"Then I would really love your help."

Harry follows the teacher into the classroom. The sharpener is on her desk, next to a big jar of pencils.

Bzzzzzzz

Bzzzzzzz

Bzzzzzzz

As Harry sharpens, kids come into the room and put away their backpacks. Some of them look at books on the shaggy rug. Others use pattern blocks or draw with markers. Two kids play a matching game that the teacher set out on a table.

Everyone looks busy and happy, but Harry feels busier than all of them. He is the special person who gets to do the pencils.

Chapter 2
MASON

DAY 3. FRIDAY, SEPTEMBER 7

"Don't leave me!" cries Harry, again, when Charlotte says goodbye.

"Oh, please," she says. "Are you going to do this every day?"

"Yes." He grabs Charlotte and wraps his legs around her like a monkey. He won't let her go. She will stay in the classroom all day with him. That'll be good. He'll just sit on her lap.

"I have toy horses in my pocket," says a voice. "Want to see?"

It is Mason.

"Hi," mumbles Harry.

Mason makes one of the horses say "Hi" back. It is

blue plastic with a hairy red mane. "His name is Ice Cream McGee."

That makes Harry smile. "Ice Cream McGee is a great name for a horse." Slowly he lets go of Charlotte. "Can I see?" he asks.

Mason hands Ice Cream McGee to Harry. "You can play with him if you want."

Harry nods. They go into the classroom together.

At morning meeting, Ms. Peek-Schnitzel asks the kids what they hope to learn in first grade. She writes down their answers. Lots of kids put their hands up right away, but Harry needs to think.

"I want to do handwriting," says Diamond. "'Cause I'm already good at drawing."

"I want to learn science about animals," says Mason.

"I want to be a better artist," says Kimani.

"I want to learn to tell a joke," says Wyatt.

"I want to make friends," says Abigail.

More kids raise their hands. Some want to tell time. Some want to write a story or learn to use a computer.

Ms. Peek-Schnitzel writes everything down. Harry is the last kid.

"Do you know what you want to learn in first grade?" the teacher asks him.

Harry has been thinking while the other kids answered. "How to be an expert," he says.

"An expert? What do you mean?"

"I want to know all about one thing so I can explain it to people. My mom is a nursing expert. My dad is a website expert. And my sister Charlotte is an expert at Crazy Eights."

"We are beginners in a lot of subjects in first grade," the teacher tells Harry. "But I bet you can become an expert on something by the time we're through. It'll take some work, though. Are you up for trying hard?"

Harry nods. He is up for it.

DAY 4. WEDNESDAY, SEPTEMBER 12

Everyone had a long weekend because of the Jewish new year, Rosh Hashanah. Harry ate challah bread and apples with honey, and he talked to his baba on the phone to say *Shana Tova,* which means "Happy New Year" in Hebrew. But mostly, he played his Fluff Monsters video game and did Lego; plus he helped Mommy clean. Harry got to use the vacuum and squirt the spray cleaner. Then he jumped on his bed.

Today, when Harry and Charlotte arrive at the classroom, Mason and his dad are in the hallway. "I wanted to wear my hedgehog shirt!" cries Mason. "I hate this shirt. The color looks like boogers."

"I think it's a nice shade of gray," says Mason's dad. "And look, it has a rhino on it. You look handsome, buddy. The hedgehog shirt wasn't clean." He gives Mason a hug and turns to go.

"Don't leave me!" says Mason. "My socks itch!"

Harry remembers how Mason helped him on Friday. "I know how to draw a Fluff Monster," Harry says, coming closer. "Want me to show you?"

Mason sniffs. He wipes his eyes. "Yes, please."

They go into the classroom together. They get markers and draw the fattest, purplest Fluff Monsters ever. They fill up six whole pieces of paper before it's even time for morning meeting.

DAY 5. THURSDAY, SEPTEMBER 13

Harry knows the name of every kid who sits at Goat Table: Mason, his friend who is funny. Wyatt, a boy with a loud voice. Abigail from kindergarten, who looks down at her hands a lot. Kimani, a girl who prints very neatly. And Diamond, a girl with a big laugh.

When it's time for math, Ms. Peek-Schnitzel makes an announcement: "This fall, we are going to study the number one hundred. By the time we're done, we'll all know this number so well, it will feel like a good friend. I promise."

She shows them how to write "100" on their papers. Then they count up to it together. Each kid says a number.

Aa Bb Cc Dd Ee Ff Gg Hh Ii Jj Kk Ll Mm Nn
100

Harry is number five. And number thirty. And fifty-five. And eighty.

It takes four go-rounds to get to one hundred. The teacher helps them if they're not sure what number comes next.

The kid who has the last number is Wyatt. "Number one hundred, woo-hoo!" he cries.

"I don't get why it's such a big whup," Harry whispers to Mason.

"Harry, my friend," says the teacher, "please don't whisper. I am explaining about counting by tens."

"But Wyatt was going *woo-hoo,*" says Harry.

"I get to go *woo-hoo,*" says Wyatt, "'cause I'm number one hundred."

Fine.

Harry makes a silly face at Mason.

Mason makes a silly face at Harry.

And Ms. Peek-Schnitzel doesn't notice, because silly faces don't make a single sound.

Chapter 3
MS. PEEK-SCHNITZEL

DAY 6. FRIDAY, SEPTEMBER 14

At the center of Goat Table is a plastic box of bead wires. Each wire has ten orange beads on it. The kids use them for counting.

Harry counts to ten, five times.

Then he tries counting backward.

Then he makes a square with four bead wires. And a triangle with three.

He pretends his bead wire is a sword. Ooh, that's more fun.

He stabs Mason, just a little bitty stab.

Mason grins and stabs back.

Sword fight! Slash, cut, cut, poke!

Ms. Peek-Schnitzel comes over. She coughs on

purpose. "Mr. Harry, Mr. Mason. Bead wires are not for battles."

That makes Harry and Mason laugh, even though the teacher is serious.

"Friends?" says Ms. Peek-Schnitzel. "I'm going to try changing our seating a bit. Okay?" She is nice about it, but she makes Harry trade seats with Amira. Now Harry sits at Rabbit Table. "I think we'll all learn better this way," she says.

For the rest of the day, Harry does not see the tiny horses Mason keeps in his pocket. Or the big smile Diamond always has on her face. He does not hear the sniffy noises Abigail makes during silent reading or the drumming Wyatt does when he is thinking.

He misses Goat Table.

Ms. Peek-Schnitzel is a big mean guinea pig, Harry thinks. She is not a nice teacher at all.

DAY 7. MONDAY, SEPTEMBER 17

Over the weekend, Harry played with Mason. He even met Mason's dog, Pebble. Pebble is a Yorkipoo. She is very small and hairy. Mason has a big bin of Legos and a whole collection of Lego people; plus his dad made grilled cheese. The whole afternoon was awesome, and now Harry and Mason are best friends.

"Can I go back to Goat Table?" Harry asks the teacher right after morning meeting.

"Aren't you happy at Rabbit?" says Ms. Peek-

Schnitzel. "I think that might be a good place for you to do your best learning."

"Goat Table, please and thank you."

"Hmm." The teacher looks thoughtful. "How about you do really good listening all day today? If everything goes well, I'll move you back to Goat."

Harry says okay, but he is frustrated. He asked super nicely and she didn't say yes. She is such a strict teacher!

He doesn't talk to anyone at Rabbit Table.

During math, he counts his bead wires quietly and thinks mean things about rabbits. How they're so hoppity and only eat vegetables. Goats are much better.

He doesn't put his hand up for help during reading, even though he is stuck on a bunch of hard words. He knows you're supposed to look at the pictures to help you, but the book just shows a girl and a blob in a bowl. The blob might be pudding, or cake batter, or soup, or even a magic potion. It's a mystery. Also, he can't figure out silent *E*.

Harry plays at recess, but he mopes all through

story time, social studies, and even music and writing. He hopes Ms. Peek-Schnitzel will notice how miserable he is. Then she'll feel sorry for scolding him on Friday.

But she does not. She doesn't seem to feel sorry.

DAY 8. TUESDAY, SEPTEMBER 18

"Harry, you were a super listener yesterday," says Ms. Peek-Schnitzel right after morning meeting. "We didn't have any problems, did we?"

What Harry wants to say is "I had a problem! I missed Goat Table. I don't even have friends at Rabbit Table." But instead, he just shakes his head no.

"I am putting you back at Goat Table," says the teacher. "I expect great behavior from you. Are you ready?"

"I'm ready," says Harry.

He is worried, though. There is so much sitting still in first grade. It is hard to be a super listener all the time, when his friends are being funny.

During writing, Ms. Peek-Schnitzel introduces the

children to her Sight Word Wall. It is a list of words the students will learn to recognize. She writes on a big sheet of lined paper: *yes, no, me,* and *you.* The class reads:

Yes, no!
Me, you!
Yes, no!
Me, you!

Diamond raises her hand. "Is it a poem?" she asks.

"Not really," says the teacher.

"Yes, no! Me, you! I sneeze. A-choo!" says Diamond.

Hee hee! "Now it's a poem," whispers Harry.

"Diamond and Harry, please don't talk while I'm teaching," says Ms. Peek-Schnitzel.

"Sometimes I think she's a stinky pants," whispers Harry to Diamond.

"Me too," whispers Diamond. "But then other times I like her."

"Excuse me, my friends," says the teacher. "What did I just tell you?"

"Not to talk while you're teaching," mumbles Harry. He stays quiet for the rest of the lesson.

DAY 9. WEDNESDAY, SEPTEMBER 19

Today is science with Mr. Daryl for the first time. Mr. Daryl doesn't look anything like the scientists in cartoons. He has a short ponytail and big muscles. He wears track pants and rubs his hands together a lot when he's excited. His science room has field mice and tiny turtles.

Mr. Daryl tells the kids they're going to study apples. He assigns each student a partner. Harry is with Abigail. He hasn't talked to Abigail much, even though she sits at his table.

Now Mr. Daryl gives each kid a red apple. "Don't eat them," he says. "We are going to cut them in half." He asks everyone to draw on small whiteboards. "What do you think you will see when I cut your apples?"

Harry draws an apple with ten seeds in it. He knows apples have seeds.

Abigail draws an apple with an apple tree inside it.

"You *really* think there will be an apple tree inside your apple?" asks Harry.

Abigail wrinkles her nose. "I hope so."

Mr. Daryl stops at their work space. He cuts Harry's apple in half from top to bottom, starting with the stem. Abigail's gets cut through the center.

There is no apple tree inside. The insides look different, cut different ways. Harry's has a round shape, and in it, he can see four brown seeds. Abigail's has five seeds, all meeting together in the center.

"It's not a tree. But it looks like a flower," says Abigail.

"It does," says Harry, in wonder.

"I love my apple!" cries Abigail.

"Mine is uglier," says Harry.

"So let's eat yours and keep mine for a treasure," says Abigail.

"Okay." They take bites from opposite sides of Harry's ugly apple.

"Don't eat your apples yet," calls out Mr. Daryl. "We're going to draw them."

"Oh, no!" whispers Abigail. "We bit ours."

Harry raises his hand. "If we bit ours, can we just draw the bites?"

"Sure," says Mr. Daryl. "That's okay, I guess."

Harry and Abigail draw the beautiful apple and the bitten, ugly one, showing the insides of the fruit and the seeds. When they write their names on their papers, Abigail shows Harry how to put a smiley face on the inside of the *a* in his name.

And just like that, Harry has a new friend.

DAY 10. THURSDAY, SEPTEMBER 20

For math, Ms. Peek-Schnitzel gives each table ten clothespins. The kids drop all ten into a bowl from up high.

How many clothespins land in the bowl? And how many land out of it?

The members of Goat Table keep a record on a piece of paper. Diamond and Wyatt take turns dropping. Kimani and Mason are counting. Harry is writing.

Six pins in and four pins out makes ten.

Three pins in and seven pins out makes ten.

Crash! go the pins.

Where is Abigail? Harry suddenly realizes she is not helping.

Crash! go the pins, again.

Oh, look. She is under the table. Her hands are over her ears.

Harry feels bad for Abigail. He knows she doesn't like loud noises. He hands the paper to Kimani and climbs under Goat Table, too. "Hi, Abigail," he says. "Want me to cover your ears for you?"

Abigail doesn't say anything. She turns away and crawls underneath Cow Table.

The classroom gets louder.

Wyatt and Mason start throwing clothespins at each other. Over at Sheep Table, Isabella and Maddie are putting the pins in each other's hair.

Suddenly, Ms. Peek-Schnitzel claps her hands three times. "One two three, eyes on me!"

"One and two, eyes on you!" the kids shout back.

"I can see clothespins on Isabella's head," the teacher

says. "And some people are throwing their pins, not drop-ping them nicely into the bowl. Also Harry and Abigail are under the tables."

Oh, no. Is Ms. Peek-Schnitzel going to scold Harry *again*?

"My friends," the teacher continues, "we are going to take a break from clothespins." She turns on the SMART Board and puts up a list. She reads it out loud.

March in place to the count of ten

Ten jumping jacks

Run in place to the count of ten

Ten jumps in place

Ten hops in place

Ten knee lifts

Ten toe-touches

Ten arm curls

Ten arm shakes

Twist in place to the count of ten

"What is this?" she asks the students.

"It's a poem," says Diamond.

The teacher looks surprised. "Well, yes," she says. "It could be. It's also a list of one hundred exercises, ten sets of ten. Do you think you can do one hundred exercises?"

"Yes!" they shout.

And they do. They do one hundred exercises, all together. All except Abigail, who opts to stay under Cow Table.

Then they fall on the rug because they are so tired.

Chapter 4
DIAMOND

DAY 11. FRIDAY, SEPTEMBER 21

The cafeteria is in the basement of the Graham School. It's painted pale green and has long tables and tiny windows. First grade and fourth grade eat at the same time, so Harry always looks for Charlotte. When he sees her, he waves, but the two grades aren't allowed to sit together. Harry sits with his friends.

Every Friday is Pizza Friday. Almost nobody brings lunch on Pizza Fridays, because pizza is delicious! Harry waits in line to get cheese pizza, fruit cocktail, and a carton of milk.

"Yummy yum," he says as he sits down with his tray.

"Yummy yum, too," says Diamond, slurping her milk.

"Yummy yum yum," says Mason.

"Yum," says Abigail.

"Hey," Harry says. "Maybe I could become a pizza-eating expert. That could be my first-grade expert thing!" He is only half joking.

"That's not a school kind of expert," says Kimani. "That's like, a thing you do on weekends."

"Watch this," says Diamond. She rips off her pizza crust and shoves the whole thing in her mouth at once.

Wow.

Harry rips off his own crust. He tries to get it into his mouth, but it won't fit.

It's too much to chew. Oof. Urgh.

Harry spits the crust into his napkin.

Maybe he won't try to be a pizza-eating expert after all.

DAY 12. MONDAY, SEPTEMBER 24

At morning meeting, Ms. Peek-Schnitzel tells the students they will be counting the first one hundred days of school. "Today is the twelfth day," she says. "On the one hundredth day, we'll have a party."

"Yay!" cries Diamond.

"Can I bring marshmallows?" asks Wyatt.

"You can bring one hundred marshmallows," says Ms. Peek-Schnitzel. "Or one hundred paper clips. Or one hundred stickers. Everyone will bring one hundred *somethings*."

Now it is time to talk about classroom jobs. "You'll get a job today, and you'll keep that job for a couple of weeks, at least," explains the teacher.

Harry's job is Calendar. That means that today he writes the number twelve in the correct square in the blank calendar on the wall.

Calendar is a terrible job. It's just writing in a square.

A baby could write in a square.

Okay, a baby could not write in a square. But Harry wants to be Line Leader, like Diamond. Line Leader gets to be at the front of every single line.

Diamond lifts her chin high walking to music. Everyone is behind her as they go downstairs, past the main office with the rows of mail cubbies, past the security guard in her neat blue uniform, to the auditorium.

"How come you get to be Line Leader?" Harry whispers, sitting down.

"I'm good at being in line," Diamond whispers back.

"I'm good at it, too."

"No you're not. You're always talking to Mason."

Yeah, that does happen. Lining up is super boring, that's why.

"That's 'cause Mason is my best friend," explains Harry. "But I'd be quiet if I got to be Line Leader."

The auditorium is a big room with a stage and wooden chairs that are bolted to the floor. Music class happens on the stage, where there is a piano. Ms. Boggs, the music teacher, says hello and shows them her accordion. She has a barky voice and sleek, short hair. She holds the accordion between her hands and squeezes it in and out to make a moaning noise. Then she adds fingers on the keyboard and plays a song.

Harry knows that song! It's "Row, Row, Row Your Boat."

Ms. Boggs tells them there is a long history of boat songs and songs about the ocean. They will be learning some of them in first grade. They sing "Row, Row, Row Your Boat," and then she teaches them a new song.

Cape Cod girls ain't got no combs—
Heave away, haul away!
They comb their hair with codfish bones!
Bound away for Australia!

Cape Cod kids ain't got no sleds—
Heave away, haul away!
They slide down hills on codfish heads!
Bound away for Australia!

The teacher adds in the accordion, and they all sing it again.

Harry remembers that Charlotte told him Ms. Boggs is the teacher who yells sometimes. But she isn't yelling now. She is making music!

DAY 13. TUESDAY, SEPTEMBER 25

During math, Ms. Peek-Schnitzel hands out charts with one hundred squares on them. Ten rows of ten. There are numbers inside the squares. She says, "Color in all the nines, my friends."

Harry wants to color with the green pencil, but Diamond takes it first.

"You can have blue," she says, when he complains.

Fine. Who cares?

Harry colors all his nines with the blue pencil. They make a stripe up his paper.

He keeps coloring and thinks:

Diamond is a booger head
Diamond is a booger head
I don't LIKE her, not at all!
'Cause Diamond is a booger head.

Diamond sits next to him, still coloring in green. "I thought of a poem and you can't hear it," Harry tells her.

"Please?" she says.

"Nope."

"Pretty please, tell me the poem?"

"No way," he says.

Diamond raises her hand. "Ms. Peek-Schnitzel! Harry thought of a poem and now he won't let me hear it."

Uh-oh.

The teacher comes over. "Do you want to share your poem, Harry?"

Harry's face feels hot. "Nuh-uh."

"Then why did he tell me he had a poem?" whines Diamond. "He shouldn't say that and then say I can't hear it. It's like saying you have candy and you won't share."

"It's not exactly the same," says Ms. Peek-Schnitzel. "A poem might be personal or private."

Diamond huffs. "I'm going to finish my nines and not think any more about this disaster," she says.

DAY 14. WEDNESDAY, SEPTEMBER 26

In science, they taste-test red, yellow, and green apples. Mr. Daryl has cut them into chunks. "Which one do you like best?" he asks. He writes the question on the white-board with his muscly arms.

"Green ones for sure, because green is my favorite color," says Diamond as they sample the apples.

"It's my favorite color, too, but color isn't the same as yummy," says Harry.

"It is to me."

"Did you even taste the red and yellow ones?"

"I don't need to. I only like green."

"Why are you even talking to me?" says Harry. "You tell me I talk too much in line, and now you talk too much in class."

"Nuh-uh."

"Yah-huh."

Mr. Daryl polls the class: "Which one was the most delicious?" He draws a chart that shows the results. Most people picked yellow, like Harry. It was the sweet-est. A few people liked red, and one person liked green.

"I'm the only one who liked green apples best," says Diamond to Kimani as they line up to go back to Ms. Peek-Schnitzel's classroom. "I win!"

Kimani high-fives Diamond.

"Tasting is not a winning thing," says Harry. "There wasn't a winner."

"There was too a winner," says Diamond. "And why are you always talking in line?"

DAY 15. THURSDAY, SEPTEMBER 27

After playtime, morning meeting, math, and reading, it is always time to line up for lunch.

Today, Harry has a peanut-butter sandwich plus canned peaches, applesauce, and a box of raisins.

Blech. That is what his mom packs when there's not much in the house.

Diamond is leading the line right in front of him. She peeks into her lunch bag. "Leftover pasta with meatballs, hooray!"

Then it's time to go downstairs, and Diamond lifts her chin high again, all proud to be the Line Leader.

Harry pushes her as they start to walk. Just a little push. She is not walking fast enough. Also, he is totally tired of her.

"Stop!" says Diamond.

And Harry pushes her again. A little harder than before.

Ms. Peek-Schnitzel turns. "We need to have a serious talk, Mr. Harry," she says.

How did she see what happened? Does she have eyeballs in the back of her head?

Everyone walks to the cafeteria, where the lunch aides watch the kids. Ms. Peek-Schnitzel makes Harry stay in the hall with her.

They sit down on two hard chairs. She lets him start eating his yucky sandwich and talks about how hands are not for pushing. "If you are angry at your friend, that's okay," says the teacher. "Everyone gets angry sometimes. Our job in first grade is to say how we feel with words."

Harry knows that. He is sorry he pushed Diamond. But he does not know how to say how he feels in words. If he tried, it would come out "Thinks-she-won-the-apples-bragged-about-a-yummy-lunch-didn't-share-the-green-pencil-pizza-expert-Line-Leader-booger-head!"

He knows those are not the words Ms. Peek-Schnitzel wants to hear. She wants organized words and nothing about boogers.

So he doesn't say any words at all. He just stares at the floor and bites his thumb.

"Do you want to tell me how you're feeling about Diamond?" Ms. Peek-Schnitzel asks, after a minute.

"No." Harry can't look her in the eye.

"Okay. Well. Can you use words in the future, instead of pushing?"

Harry nods.

"Great. It was nice to have this talk with you, Harry," says the teacher. "You may go to lunch now. I'll see you after."

As he heads into the cafeteria, Harry thinks that she did all the talking, really.

DAY 16. FRIDAY, SEPTEMBER 28

When you're Calendar, there *is* one special part of the job: you get to lead a song about the days of the week.

Ms. Peek-Schnitzel had been waiting to introduce it, but today she taught it to Harry privately first thing when he got to school. Now he stands up in front of everyone and leads them.

What is today? Friday, Friday.

What was yesterday? Thursday, Thursday.

What is tomorrow? Saturday, Saturday.

Harry points at the different days on the calendar with a stick. The other kids are watching him! Calendar is not such a bad job after all.

Diamond raises her hand. "It's a poem," she says.

"Nuh-uh," calls out Wyatt. "It's a song."

"It's a poem *and* a song," says Diamond.

Later, during writing time, the teacher asks, "What rules should we all follow in school?" She has everybody brainstorm answers on their paper, without worrying about spelling. When they are finished, she has them share their best ideas.

"Don't throw the clothespins," says Jayden.

"Don't go under the table," says Abigail.

"Come to school on time," says Mason.

"Don't pick your boogers," says Wyatt. Everyone laughs.

"Let's be serious," says Ms. Peek-Schnitzel.

"I am serious," says Wyatt. "You really shouldn't pick them."

"Don't bully people," says Adam.

"Or say mean stuff about their families," adds Orlando.

"Share the green pencil if somebody wants it," says Harry.

"Don't push the Line Leader," says Diamond.

Harry knows she is right. "Sorry about that," he whispers.

"It's okay," Diamond whispers back. "Sorry I didn't share the pencil."

DAY 17. MONDAY, OCTOBER 1

Harry and Charlotte are walking to school. Just the two of them, without their mom. It feels very grown-up. The ginkgo trees have turned bright yellow, the way they do every autumn. Leaves sprinkle the sidewalk, all down the block. There are ginkgo berries on the ground, too. They smell like farts.

Harry decides to collect the pretty yellow leaves for his classroom. He wants to bring one hundred!

"Hurry up," says Charlotte. "We'll be late."

But Harry is counting leaves.

When he puts all one hundred leaves on her desk, Ms. Peek-Schnitzel gives Harry a huge smile. Even though he *is* late.

The students make ginkgo-leaf rubbings. They put the leaves bumpy side up, set paper on top of them, and roll the long sides of crayons hard across the bumps. Leaf shapes turn up on their papers, like magic.

Harry moves his leaves and rubs his paper over and over so it looks like there are lots of leaves all across it. He uses a million colors. "I made rainbow leaves!" he says.

"You need green to make a rainbow," says Diamond.

"They're not rainbow leaves unless you have green." She looks down at the green crayon in her hand. It is the only green crayon at Goat Table. She hands it to Harry. "Here, you take a turn."

And Harry does.

Chapter 5
FAMILY CIRCLES

DAY 18. TUESDAY, OCTOBER 2

The students have library with Ms. Tellicherry on Tuesdays. Ms. Tellicherry has thick hair she wears in a ponytail, and a long oval face. She reminds Harry of a friendly horse. Today, she's wearing a fuzzy brown sweater.

The librarian has already shown the kids where to find fiction picture books and nonfiction picture books on the shelves. Now she brings them to her special storytime area that looks like a wooden ship. It has a pretend sail and everything.

"Get on board!" she says in her librarian whisper.

Inside the make-believe ship, the kids sit on three levels of risers covered with brown carpet. Ms. Tellicherry sits by the ship's wheel and reads a book about a kid on a bus with his grandma.

Wyatt puts his hand up. "I live with my grandma, too," he says.

"Where's your mom?" Diamond asks.

Wyatt shrugs. "That's who I live with."

Harry puts his hand up, but other people are shouting out.

"I live with my mom, my dad, and my brothers," says Kimani.

"I live with Mom and Mama," says Diamond.

"I live with six dogs," says Abigail softly. Then she giggles. Harry wonders if she is joking. Or pretending.

"I wish *I* lived with six dogs," says Mason.

"We'll talk about our families tomorrow," says Ms. Peek-Schnitzel. "Right now it's time for everyone to choose a book. Right, Ms. Tellicherry?"

Harry finds a book that shows a boy in a wrestling costume on the cover. Inside are pictures of weird silly monsters. It looks so fun! He is totally taking it home.

DAY 19. WEDNESDAY, OCTOBER 3

The teacher asks about people's families. "I live with my husband, Carl, and my mother," she tells them.

"Where are your children?" asks Mia.

"They're grown and moved away."

Harry puts his hand up. "I live with my mom and my sister," he tells the class.

He wants to explain that his dad lives far away in Boston, and that he can't even remember when Daddy used to live with them. But there isn't time, because Amira calls out, "I live with my mom and dad."

"I live with my dad and my sister," says Jayden. "And then with my mom and my sister when it's a different week."

"I live with Mom, Papa, and my dog, Pebble," says Mason. "And my birth mother lives in Ethiopia."

Some kids live with only one grown-up. Some live with two or even three. Elijah has a pet ferret. Isabella has a sister and a foster mom and dad, plus a mom. Orlando has two dads.

"That's weird," Elijah says to Orlando.

"Not any weirder than a ferret," says Diamond.

"Yeah," says Orlando.

"Ferrets aren't weird," says Elijah.

"Nobody's family is weird. All families are just families," says Ms. Peek-Schnitzel. Her voice sounds final.

"What about ferrets?" asks Diamond.

"It would be more accurate to say that ferrets are *unusual* pets here in Brooklyn," says the teacher.

DAY 20. THURSDAY, OCTOBER 4

During morning meeting, Ms. Peek-Schnitzel tapes a large sheet of paper to the wall over the book bins. "This will be our Sparkly Word Wall," she says. "It's different from our Sight Word Wall. These words will make our conversations and our stories sparkle! You can use these words even if you can't spell them yet."

She writes the word *weird* on the Sparkly Word Wall.

Then she writes *usual* and *unusual*. "*Weird* means 'spooky' or 'strange,' but *unusual* just means 'uncommon, not ordinary.'" She sounds out the word: "Un-*yoo*-zyoo-ul."

"It's okay to be weird," says Abigail. "My mom says it takes all types to make the world."

Ms. Peek-Schnitzel nods. "I agree. But *weird* can be a hurtful word sometimes."

"I think *un*-yoo-*zyoo-ul* is different from *weird*," says

Elijah, saying the long new word carefully. "Ferrets are unusual pets but not weird pets."

Harry raises his hand. "Cheese puffs are weird if you think about them too much," he says. "But they're usual."

Everyone is silent for a moment, considering cheese puffs.

Harry thinks he might like the Sparkly Word Wall quite a lot. Without it, he wouldn't have had that idea about puffs. And now everyone in the class is thinking about it.

DAY 21. FRIDAY, OCTOBER 5

During social studies, the students make family circle charts. Each kid puts a small circle in the middle of the paper. Inside that circle goes the kid's name.

Around that goes a circle for names of other kids in the family.

Around that goes a circle for the grown-ups.

Around that goes a circle for the old people.

"However many parents you want to put, that's fine,"

says the teacher. "If you have important people who live far away, put down their names, too. And if you want to put down cousins, godparents, or anyone else, do it. It's all good."

Elijah raises his hand. "What about my ferret?"

Mason puts his hand up. "What about my dog?"

"Let's just put humans," says Ms. Peek-Schnitzel.

"But my ferret is important to me!" says Elijah.

"So is my dog!" says Mason.

"So are my six dogs," says Abigail softly.

"Okay, fine." Ms. Peek-Schnitzel sighs. "You can put pets in the same circle as kids."

Harry's chart has him at the center. In the kid circle

he puts Charlotte. In the grown-up circle he writes Mommy and Daddy, and then his mother's brother, Uncle Stevie. He adds Evaline, his babysitter.

In the old-people circle he puts Baba and Grandpa Mike, Great-Aunt Irina, Grandpa Cillian, and Nana.

Abigail has put six dog names in the kid circle. She reads them to Harry, since the words are tricky. "Tally, Puddleduck, Bacon, Eggs, Scooter, and Toad," says Abigail.

"Do you really have six dogs?" whispers Harry.

Abigail nods, but one corner of her mouth turns up. Harry is still not sure whether to believe her.

Wyatt's grown-up circle says *Mom* but not *Dad*. His old-people circle has a bunch of names. Harry is curious, but he remembers what Ms. Peek-Schnitzel said: "All families are just families." So he doesn't ask.

DAY 22. TUESDAY, OCTOBER 9

Yesterday was a holiday. Nobody went to school.

Harry went to Mason's apartment. They played with

Pebble. Mason's mom took them to the park. Then they ate spaghetti.

Today, Ms. Peek-Schnitzel explains about the day off. "It has traditionally been called Columbus Day, but change makers in more and more places are renaming it Indigenous People's Day."

"How come?" asks Harry.

"Columbus was a famous explorer who traveled from Spain a long time ago, in 1492." She shows them on the map. "He landed in what's now Haiti, North America. But his arrival led to sad and terrible things for the people who were already living there, and in the rest of North America." She points on the map. "Renaming the day honors the first people of this land, the Indigenous or First Nations people. *Indigenous* means that people come from this land and have always been here." She says students at the Graham School will study this history in fourth grade. She shows them another map. "Here you can see the names of indigenous groups and their territories from that time. The Lenape are from the New York City area, where we live now."

After lunch, Ms. Peek-Schnitzel writes the word *indigenous* on the Sparkly Word Wall. "Does anyone know if your family members are indigenous Americans?"

Robbie raises his hand. Lots of kids shrug. They aren't sure.

"If your family isn't indigenous, that means they came here from somewhere else at some point in time. Remember the people in your family circles?" Ms. Peek-Schnitzel points to the wall where they are taped up. "Did your parents or other important adults grow up far away from the USA? Raise your hand if they did."

A bunch of kids put up their hands. Others seem unsure. Harry raises his hand because his father came from Ireland.

"Great. Hands down. Now, are your old people, grandparents and so on, from far away?" says Ms. Peek-Schnitzel. "Raise your hand if they are."

Hands go up. Harry puts his up because Nana and Grandpa Cillian still live in Ireland, and Baba came from Ukraine.

"Thank you. Hands down. Now, even *you* might have come from far away, when you were little. Do you know if you did?"

Mason, Orlando, and Maddie put their hands up.

"My grandparents came here from Poland and Germany," says Ms. Peek-Schnitzel.

Mason waves his hand. "My dog came from New Jersey," he says.

Chapter 6
WYATT

DAY 23. WEDNESDAY, OCTOBER 10

This morning, as Harry hangs up his jacket in the cubby area, Wyatt looms over him. He's humongous, and his eyeballs bulge. "I'm gonna pull your pants down!" Wyatt whispers.

"What? No!"

"Yes!"

"Don't!" Harry says, giggling. "Don't!" He's laughing, but he doesn't think it's funny.

Wyatt reaches out and snaps Harry's waistband.

Harry looks around for Ms. Peek-Schnitzel. She is talking to Mr. Daryl, who stands in the doorway.

"Don't!" Harry giggles again without wanting to.

"Nah, it's just a joke," says Wyatt, sauntering away. "I wasn't really going to do it."

Harry puts his jacket back on and doesn't take it off for the rest of the day.

DAY 24. THURSDAY, OCTOBER 11

Harry wears a belt to school to keep his pants secure. He watches Wyatt.

Will Wyatt snap his waistband again? Or even worse, try to pull down his pants?

At recess, Harry is scared Wyatt will come up behind

him. He doesn't play on top of the Rocket with Mason. Instead, he sits against the brick wall.

But Wyatt doesn't snap Harry's pants.

In fact, the whole day goes by without Wyatt even saying anything about pants. Yay! Harry breathes easily again.

DAY 25. FRIDAY, OCTOBER 12

Harry doesn't like his belt. The buckle is too tricky, so it's hard to use the toilet. So today, he didn't wear it.

He is waiting in line for pizza, when up comes Wyatt and snaps his waistband. "I'm gonna pull your pants down," Wyatt says, grinning.

Harry does that nervous laugh again, without meaning to. He clutches his pants. When he gets his pizza, he keeps a grip on his waistband with one hand and carefully holds his tray with the other. And when everyone goes outdoors for recess, he sits with his back against the wall.

"I don't like Wyatt," Harry tells his babysitter,

Evaline, after school. Evaline is a tall, narrow person with a warm voice and an even warmer smile. She has grown-up children already and is very good at making mac and cheese. Harry likes when she takes him and Charlotte to the park in the afternoons, but some days they have to run errands instead. Today, they are picking up groceries and dry-cleaning for Harry's mom, who is at work till nine o'clock.

"What's wrong with Wyatt?" asks Evaline.

"He's a meanie," says Harry.

"What flavor of mean?"

"He teases. Like, he says I never lost a tooth but he lost one already, ha ha."

"Well, you told me you didn't like Diamond a couple weeks ago, and now you've had two playdates with her. Isn't that right, H?"

"Yeah."

"So maybe that will happen with Wyatt, too," says Evaline comfortingly. "Sometimes we come around to liking people."

"No way," says Harry.

"Just maybe," says Evaline. "That's all I'm saying."

But Harry is certain that Evaline is wrong.

"I like people who don't pull pants down," he says. "My pants are nobody else's business."

DAY 26. MONDAY, OCTOBER 15

Jobs change today. Wyatt gets to be Line Leader. Diamond's new job is Paper Passer. Mason is Book Bin Monitor. Kimani is Calendar. Abigail is Electrician, which means she gets to turn the lights off when they leave the room.

Harry's job is Plant Manager. He is supposed to check the classroom plants to see if they need water. If the dirt is dry, he waters them.

The plants are ugly and brownish green.

Who wants to be Plant Manager?

No one in a million years, that's who. No one in all of Brooklyn, thinks Harry.

"Can I switch to Line Leader?" he asks Ms. Peek-Schnitzel at the end of the day.

"My friend, you know there is no switching jobs."

"What if Wyatt *wants* to switch?"

"There is just no switching. Everyone will change jobs in about a month anyway."

"What if Wyatt loves plants so much? Because I think he loves plants. I think maybe he told me he loves ferns and other planty things. Yes."

"Just stick with your job," says the teacher. "You might grow to like it."

"What if I switch with Kimani? I could go back to Calendar."

At this, Ms. Peek-Schnitzel ruffles his hair. "There is just no switching, no switching, no switching, my persistent friend Harry Bergen-Murphy," she says. "Do you know what *persistent* means?"

"Annoying?" Charlotte calls Harry annoying sometimes.

"No, no. It's a compliment," says Ms. Peek-Schnitzel. "*Persistent* means to continue trying even when things aren't going your way. You're very persistent, and I admire that."

"So . . ."

"So there is still no switching," says Ms. Peek-Schnitzel.

DAY 27. TUESDAY, OCTOBER 16

All first graders at the Graham School study Self and Community. That's why Ms. Peek-Schnitzel's students made self-portraits and drew family circles. Today they go on a neighborhood walk. It is bright and sunny outside.

The teacher talks to the kids about shop owners and community workers. She points out the trees along the sidewalks: ginkgoes, northern red oaks, and crabapples. "Crabapple trees have always lived in Brooklyn," she tells them. "But the ginkgo trees were brought over from China. Crabapples are *indigenous* plants. Remember our sparkly word? Ginkgo trees are not indigenous."

Three parents go on the walk with the class: Kimani's mom, Orlando's papa, and Robbie's mom.

They pass the firehouse and see a real fire engine. They pass a bus stop and watch the city bus drive by. The last stop is a visit to D'Angelo's bakery, owned by Ms. Peek-Schnitzel's friend Gina D'Angelo. Ms. D'Angelo shows the kids her bakery kitchen. There are racks for the trays of cookies and a whole wall of ovens. Huge silver mixers stand in a row. They look even more fun to use than the electric pencil sharpener.

After the tour, Ms. D'Angelo lets them taste samples. Harry tastes an Italian lace cookie, a rainbow cookie, and an anisette. The anisette is yuck. He sneaks a second lace cookie.

"Maybe I could be a cookie-baking expert," says Harry, chewing.

"Great idea," says Mason. "I would love if you were a cookie-baking expert. 'Cause I could help eat the cookies!"

"And I would give you cookies, 'cause we are best friends," says Harry.

Wyatt shakes his head. "You can't do that in first grade," he says. "It's like dangerous mixing machines and hot ovens."

"I help my mom bake cookies," says Harry.

"Everybody does *that*," says Wyatt. "That's not an expert."

"I could be an expert at *eating* cookies," says Harry.

"You are already," says Mason, pointing to the partly eaten lace cookie in Harry's hand. "You bit it, you chewed it, you swallowed it. You're an expert!"

"Nuh-uh," says Wyatt. "Anyone can eat cookies."

On the way home, Mason and Harry walk together. It doesn't matter that Wyatt is acting all proud to be Line Leader. Mason and Harry don't need him.

He's not even their friend.

DAY 28. WEDNESDAY, OCTOBER 17

Halloween is coming. In Harry's neighborhood, grown-ups will sit on the steps of their homes with bowls full of candy for trick-or-treaters. Before the holiday, they decorate their buildings with pretend spider webs and spooky plastic statues.

Harry's mother put four big pumpkins on the steps of their apartment building. A neighbor taped a paper skeleton to their front door. Another neighbor put out a white blow-up ghost and a bunch of orange lights. Now Harry's building looks very Halloweeny!

Mommy will be a butterfly. She wears the same pair of wings every year, on top of her coat. Charlotte will be a vampire. And Harry has thought of the best Halloween costume. He's going to be Gar-Gar, the black-and-yellow Fluff Monster!

Yesterday after school, Evaline took Harry and Charlotte on the subway to a fabric store. They bought two colors of thick, hairy fluff material. Mommy will sew them together to make Gar-Gar.

Today Harry has some of his fluff in his backpack to show to Mason, Diamond, and Abigail. He gets it out at recess.

"Let's *all* be Fluff Monsters!" shouts Diamond.

Yes!

Mason can be Boompus, the purple Fluff Monster.

Diamond can be Gorf, the green one.

Abigail can be Dumpler, who is red and orange.

It is the best idea in the world.

DAY 29. THURSDAY, OCTOBER 18

Mason has already gotten his Fluff Monster fluff. During morning playtime, he shows a tiny piece to Harry. It is so purple!

Wyatt comes over to the cubby area where they are standing. "Is that for your Halloween costume?" he asks.

Mason explains. "Harry, me, Diamond, and Abigail—we're all trick-or-treating together. We're being Fluff Monsters."

"Whatever," says Wyatt. "*Fluff Monsters* is for babies."

Harry wants to push Wyatt for saying that. It makes him super mad, because *Fluff Monsters* is important to him.

He clenches his fists and keeps them by his side. "I don't want *you* to be a Fluff Monster anyway," he tells Wyatt. "It's just for me, Mason, Diamond, and Abigail. No one else."

Wyatt's face crumples.

He turns and walks away.

DAY 30. FRIDAY, OCTOBER 19

Today for math, the teacher gives each table one hundred Dixie cups. The children line them up in rows of ten. Ten rows of ten make a square.

"Now, what can you build together?" she asks.

One group builds a swimming pool. Another tries to make a bus. The kids at Goat Table agree to build a castle.

Harry stacks the cups so their rims touch. He and Mason build tall, wobbly towers. Abigail makes a castle wall. Kimani draws on two of the cups and cuts them with scissors so the cups have wings. Then she does things with tape. The cups look like dragons!

Diamond copies her and makes some castle chickens.

Wyatt tries to make a dragon, too, but it ends up mangled.

"Maybe it's a castle slug," says Harry.

"It's not a slug," says Wyatt.

"It could be a slug if you cut the wings off," says Harry. He goes back to putting a cup on the tippy-top of his tall tower.

"No it can't!" snaps Wyatt, and sweeps his arm across the table.

The castle towers fall.

The castle walls fall.

The castle dragons and the castle chickens fall.

"You ruined it!" cries Harry.

"So what?" yells Wyatt.

"We should have taped the towers," says Kimani.

"And the wall," says Abigail.

"We should have taped everything," says Kimani.

Diamond cries because Mason has stepped on one of her chickens by accident. Now it is a flat chicken. Mason picks up Dixie cups from the floor.

Ms. Peek-Schnitzel comes over and helps the kids clean up. "Sometimes projects like these are frustrating," she tells Wyatt. "We are all learning to work together. That's part of the experience."

But Wyatt begins to cry. He cries without putting his hands over his face, just shaking and whimpering while his cheeks get wet.

The teacher gets people settled with bins of books

for reading and takes Wyatt into the reading area to talk quietly. She gives him a box of tissues and pats him gently on the back.

Harry tries to sound out the words in his book, but they're hard and he can't concentrate. Wyatt is sniffling too loud.

Chapter 7
STORYBOOK PARADE

DAY 31. MONDAY, OCTOBER 22

At the Graham School, on the day of Halloween, there will be a Storybook Parade. Students will dress in costumes inspired by characters from books. Hooray!

Harry remembers the parade from kindergarten, but the kindergartners didn't march. They only watched.

"Is a My Little Pony book okay?" asks Kimani during morning meeting. "'Cause that's a TV show."

"Is Star Wars okay?" asks Robbie.

"If it's in a book, then it's fine," says Ms. Peek-Schnitzel. "You need a copy to carry with you in the parade."

"Is Captain Underpants okay?" asks Wyatt.

Harry leans in to hear the answer. He does *not* want Wyatt thinking about underpants.

"Captain Underpants has lots of books," says the teacher, "but I don't think underpants and a cape are enough clothing for school."

"Is the Incredible Hulk okay?" asks Elijah. "He only wears pants and no shirt."

"Everyone should wear tops and bottoms, shoes and socks," says Ms. Peek-Schnitzel. "And remember, it's not a Halloween parade. Some of our Muslim friends, our Orthodox Jewish friends, and other friends here at Graham School do not celebrate Halloween. We don't bring that holiday to school."

Harry already knows he will be Gar-Gar the Fluff Monster. He will definitely have enough clothes on.

DAY 32. TUESDAY, OCTOBER 23

During reading, Abigail whispers to Mason, Diamond, and Harry. "We have a problem."

"What is it?" Harry whispers back.

"No Fluff Monster book. We need one for the parade," says Abigail.

"That's right," says Wyatt, looking up. "If you don't have a book, you can't be it. Teacher said."

Uh-oh.

They spend the rest of reading time looking through the books in the bins. They search for Fluff Monsters.

They don't find a single one.

DAY 33. WEDNESDAY, OCTOBER 24

Mr. Daryl, the science teacher, has the students float pumpkins in bins filled with water. "Indigenous people here in the Northeast grew pumpkins for food, along with many other vegetables. Nowadays, pumpkins are still an important food for the many types of people in this area. We cook pumpkin pies, soups, and muffins, especially at this time of year, the harvest season."

The little pumpkins float.

The big pumpkins float.

"That's because they're mostly hollow inside," says Mr. Daryl. "They're not as dense as the water. Later today, we can cut them open and see the insides. When we're done, I'll take them home to roast the seeds and make pies."

Everyone is pushing pumpkins down to watch them pop back up to the surface. Harry and Mason get their sleeves wet.

Then Harry dips his head in.

Hee hee. His hair gets soaked. The cool water drips down his neck and over his face.

"Your hair is *unusual*!" says Mason.

Harry rubs his head to make his hair stick up. "Now it's even unusualer."

Mason dips *his* head in. The water makes droplets all through his hair.

Harry dips his head in again.

The bin tips over. Water floods the science room.

Uh-oh.

Mr. Daryl strides over.

"He's gonna be mad," Harry whispers to Mason. "He's gonna yell. Cover your ears."

But the teacher just laughs. "Today is the first time

I ever did this project with first graders," he tells them. "Good thing I brought towels."

Mr. Daryl gives the boys towels, and they help dry the floor. When Harry looks up, he sees that Wyatt and his partner, Mia, have wet hair, too. So do Diamond and Adam. "I was really hot, but now I cooled down," says Wyatt.

Harry smiles. Wyatt's shirt is drenched and his hair is drippy. "That tub was like a tiny swimming pool," Harry says. "Right?"

"Just the right size for my head," says Wyatt. "My head or a pumpkin. Look, I'm a pumpkin head!" He takes a pumpkin and puts it in front of his face.

Sometimes Wyatt is funny, Harry has to admit.

DAY 34. THURSDAY, OCTOBER 25

Parents and caregivers have been invited to the classroom. They were told to bring seasonal snacks for the Harvest Festival. It seems like *seasonal* means "pumpkin-flavored," because like Mr. Daryl was saying, people have made pumpkin cookies, pumpkin cupcakes with cream cheese frosting, pumpkin pie, and pumpkin muffins topped with roasted pumpkin seeds.

Harry's mom brought apple cider. She is here in her hospital scrubs, which are a bright blue top and matching pants. It's a nurse's uniform. She is going to work right after this. She talks to Diamond's mama about sewing the Fluff Monster costumes, explaining how she made a fluffy hood for Harry's head. "I'm not worrying about monster feet," she says. "He'll just wear his regular shoes."

Harry gets a plate with all four pumpkin treats. He brings them to sit next to his mom on the rug.

Yuck. Yuck. Yuck. And yuck.

"Don't worry, I'll eat them for you." His mom laughs. "I like pumpkin."

"I like chocolate," says Harry.

She digs in her purse and gives him a square of milk chocolate. Harry unwraps it and moves onto her lap. The flavor floods his mouth, and his tongue finds a wiggly front tooth. It's loose!

He shows it to her even though his mouth is all chocolaty. She gives him a big squeeze.

For the rest of the day, Harry wiggles his tooth back and forth in his mouth.

Math, wiggle!

Reading, wiggle!

Recess, wiggle, wiggle, wiggle!

He feels so different, with his wiggly tooth.

DAY 35. FRIDAY, OCTOBER 26

Yesterday, Harry's mother asked Evaline to take him and Charlotte to the big public library so they could look for Fluff Monster picture books.

They looked.

And looked.

They researched on the computer. They even asked the librarian for help.

No luck.

"I'm being Harry Potter for the parade," says Kimani today at lunch. "My dad read me Book One, and anyway, my brother already had the costume."

Harry knows about those books from Charlotte. "Harry Potter is a boy," he tells Kimani. "You can't be him."

"Yes I can," says Kimani. "Harry Potter is for everybody. Didn't your parents teach you that?"

"I *have* to be a Fluff Monster," says Mason. "My dad already bought the fluff."

"Mama bought the fluff, too," says Diamond. "And started sewing. No way she's going to make a different costume."

"My whole costume is finished already," says Abigail.

So is Harry's.

But do Fluff Monster books even exist? There are only five days left until the parade.

DAY 36. MONDAY, OCTOBER 29

Harry's mom took him shopping over the weekend. There were no Fluff Monster books at the nearby bookstore. "There *has* been a book published," said the store lady, looking at her tablet. "But just one. It's called *Fluff Monster Party*. And sadly, it is out of print. I can't get it for you. I think you'll have to find it at the library."

"We already checked the library," said Harry's mom. "But thank you."

Now, on her day off and while Charlotte is at a playdate after school, Mommy takes Harry to a farther-away bookshop.

There is no Fluff Monster book there, either.

As they walk home, Harry asks if she would order it from an online bookstore.

"Let's try," she says, checking her phone.

Yes, she can buy *Fluff Monster Party,* but because the book is out of print, she can only buy it used. That means it will ship slowly from the used bookshop.

Too slowly.

There is no way Harry will get it by the day after to-morrow.

Bam! Bam! Harry stomps his feet. They are walking under Mommy's umbrella. He is hungry and cold and his feet just stop walking and start stomping instead.

Bam! Bam!

She bends down to look him in the eye. "Can you use your words?"

Harry nods but says nothing. No words come.

"Do you want to say the words out loud?"

"I'm . . . disappointed!" yells Harry. "Disappointed and mad. Plus disappointed and mad!"

A lady walking by turns to stare at him, but he doesn't care.

"We could call it D and M," says Mommy. "That might be easier to say. It could be a code between us."

"D and M!" yells Harry.

"D and M!" yells Mommy. "But listen," she says in her normal voice. "I'm sure Ms. Peek-Schnitzel will be

flexible about the storybooks when she sees how awesome your costumes are. She's a very nice teacher. I'll just tell her we had trouble finding it."

Harry is still worried, though. They're supposed to have *books*. And it's totally almost Halloween.

DAY 37. TUESDAY, OCTOBER 30

"The best thing in the world happened!" cries Abigail when Harry gets to school.

"What best thing?" asks Harry.

She grins the biggest grin. Then she pulls a *Fluff Monster Party* book out of her backpack. It has pictures of all four monsters on the cover. "Look!"

"Woo-hoo!" shouts Harry. He does his happy dance. "Now I don't have to be Beekle." Just in case he couldn't be a Fluff Monster, Mommy helped him choose a book with an easy costume. Beekle is an imaginary-friend character who looks like a round white ghost, so Harry could just wear a pillowcase with eyes cut in it.

But he really didn't *feel* like being Beekle.

"And I don't have to be Sophie and her squash," says Abigail. "Even though we already bought a squash for me to carry."

Diamond and Mason are excited, too. Mason didn't even have a parade costume. "I was just going to be like, a regular kid and find a book with a regular kid on the cover," he says.

"I was going to be *Z Is for Moose,*" Diamond tells them, "but all I got was antlers. Not a whole moose suit or anything."

All day, whenever they are together, they say, "FLUFF MONSTERS."

In line to go to library, they whisper, "FLUFF MONSTERS."

When the story is over, they whisper, "FLUFF MONSTERS."

Kimani is happy for them. She is all set with Harry Potter. Mia is going to be Harry's owl, Hedwig, so their costumes will go together.

Wyatt makes a sour face at Harry during lunch. "Fluff Monsters are for babies," he says. "If you all want to be baby things for the parade, go right ahead. I'll be Spider-Man."

Harry wants to say he likes Spider-Man, too, and what's wrong with Fluff Monsters? But he doesn't get a chance. Abigail, Diamond, and Mason just shout at Wyatt: "FLUFF MONSTERS! FLUFF MONSTERS! FLUFF MONSTERS!"

And Harry joins in.

Wyatt leaves the table.

DAY 38. WEDNESDAY, OCTOBER 31

It is Halloween and the day of the Storybook Parade.

Harry's Gar-Gar costume is hot and itchy, but he looks amazing. Abigail carries *Fluff Monster Party* in

her red-and-orange arms. Harry, Diamond, and Mason walk alongside her.

If they are able to get off work, parents come to watch. So do caregivers. Harry's mom is there, taking pictures on her phone. She promises to send a photo to Daddy.

Ms. Peek-Schnitzel is dressed as a pig. She carries a toy pug dog, plus the book *Pug Meets Pig*.

Everyone walks up the block, across the street, past the place where you get fried chicken, past the place where you get lo mein noodles, past the bodega. The shop and restaurant owners come out and wave. Some of them even clap.

The kids cross the street again and go down a block of town houses and apartment buildings, around the corner and

past D'Angelo's bakery, the toy shop with the robot in the window, the dollar store, the pizza place, and the other bodega.

Harry links arms with Diamond. They wave at the people watching. "Fluff Monsters!" calls one lady. "Excellent fluff."

DAY 39. THURSDAY, NOVEMBER 1

Harry is super tired. He stayed up way too late trick-or-treating last night with his friends and then eating take-out pizza.

Everyone else is tired, too. Abigail goes under Goat Table. Kimani falls asleep during math. Diamond falls asleep during story time. Mason looks weak and sick.

"When we got home, my dad said, 'How many pieces of candy did you eat?'" Mason explains. "And I told him four. So he let me have four more. But really I ate eighteen or thirty or maybe more than that."

"You lied to your dad?" says Harry.

"It popped out," says Mason. "I couldn't think straight

'cause of all the candy I owned. But he figured out the truth when I puked all over the bathroom floor. My parents put me in the shower while they bleach-cleaned."

"Ew."

"Yeah," says Mason. "And even worse, my dad took my bag of candy away. He put it on top of the fridge."

"That's so mean," says Harry.

"Yeah, my dad's a Halloween meanie," says Mason. "But I get to have my bag back after dinner tonight."

Chapter 8
LOSING

DAY 40. FRIDAY, NOVEMBER 2

Every Friday, Harry's class has gym. Ms. Tanaka, the gym teacher, is very strong and loud. She doesn't yell, exactly, but her voice is sharp. Still, Harry likes gym. First they do animal warm-ups. They skitter like crabs and

then tromp like bears. They hop like bunnies and skip like deer. Ms. Tanaka calls out the animals, faster and faster.

Today they learn a new game: Sharks and Minnows. There is a team of sharks and a team of minnows.

Harry is a minnow.

The idea is that the minnows run from one wall of the gym to the other while the sharks try to catch them. Once a minnow gets caught, it becomes a shark. There are more and more sharks until finally, there is only one minnow left.

Harry runs high-speed. The sharks catch Diamond first. Then Robbie and Kimani. Then Wyatt and some other kids.

Harry runs high-speed again, but now there are more sharks, so it is harder.

Wyatt tags him.

"Why are you always trying to get me?" says Harry as the sharks go back to their starting place. He didn't want to turn into a shark. He wanted to be the speediest minnow.

"'Cause you're too slow and I'm so fast," says Wyatt, shrugging. "Let's eat up Mason, 'kay?"

"I'm not eating up my best friend," says Harry.

"It's a game, doof."

Ms. Tanaka blows her whistle and the sharks are supposed to chase again.

"Ahhhh!" Harry complains. He was a minnow like, a minute ago, and now he's supposed to *eat* the minnows? It feels wrong.

"Wyatt knows what he's talking about," says Diamond before she runs off. "I've been a shark for a long time now. Just pretend you're a great white, gobble up the minnows, and that's that. No biggie."

Then Mason zips by. "Try to eat me!" he yells.

So Harry does. He chases Mason—*zoom!*—across the gym.

DAY 41. MONDAY, NOVEMBER 5

Tomorrow is Election Day. No school. Ms. Peek-Schnitzel reads the students a book about a girl named Grace who wants to be president. She writes *election* on the Sparkly Word Wall.

"It's important to vote. That way, you get a say about what goes on in the world," says the teacher. "And here in first grade, we are going to have an election, too. A pretend one. A silly one. Okay?"

"Okay!" the kids shout.

"Let's pretend we are going to elect a class president. Everybody will get to vote. And the candidates are . . . Fluff Monsters."

"Real Fluff Monsters?" asks Abigail.

"Well," says Ms. Peek-Schnitzel, "they're puppets. I'm going to do their voices."

She pulls out a puppet of Dumpler, the red-and-orange Fluff Monster. "I want to be president," she says in her Dumpler voice. "I collect gold and jewels and seashells."

Then she brings out a puppet Gorf, the green fluff monster. "I want to be president," she makes Gorf say. "I like honey, sugar, and everything sweet."

The Dumpler puppet is back. "Tell us about how you

will be a good president," says the teacher, using her regular voice.

Then she does her Dumpler voice. "I will help you with math because I am very good at counting. I can count way over one hundred. Also, I will share my seashells with you."

Ms. Peek-Schnitzel changes to the Gorf puppet. "Tell us about how *you* will be a good president," she says in her real voice.

Then she does her Gorf voice: "Cupcakes every day. Yum yum yum."

"Is there anything else important?" asks the teacher.

"Nope! Cupcakes every day. Yum yum yum," says Gorf.

Now the kids ask questions.

"If you get to be president, will you help when it's cleanup time?" asks Kimani.

Dumpler says: "I will help, but I have very short arms. Kids will need to do most of the cleanup work."

Gorf says: "Cupcakes every day. Yum yum yum."

"If you get to be president, will you be nice to us if we don't understand a lesson?" asks Abigail.

Dumpler says: "I will be nice. I will try to help you understand."

Gorf says: "Cupcakes every day. Yum yum yum."

Then Ms. Peek-Schnitzel puts the puppets away. She gives each kid an index card. "Write *Gorf* if you want Gorf to be our president. Write *Dumpler* if you want Dumpler."

Harry votes for Dumpler. Everyone turns in their cards. Ms. Peek-Schnitzel counts the votes.

Gorf wins.

Some kids cheer. They like Gorf because she is so funny. But Harry is a bit sad. So is Abigail. They are both fans of Dumpler.

DAY 42. WEDNESDAY, NOVEMBER 7

Harry went to vote with Mommy yesterday. She voted at the YMCA where they sometimes play basketball on weekends, but it looked different. It was set up with booths and tables. There was a line and they had to wait. Afterward, Mommy let Harry have her I VOTED sticker to put on his coat.

Today, lots of kids have stickers on their jackets, just

like Harry. Ms. Peek-Schnitzel admires them. "I like to see people voting, because voting is one of the ways we can be change makers in our world," she says.

They are talking about voting at morning meeting when Diamond raises her hand. "My mom ran for city council, but she didn't win," she says.

Harry doesn't know what city council is, but it sounds important. "Is she sad?" he asks.

"She cried," says Diamond. "Then I cried because she cried. Then it was my bedtime."

Ms. Peek-Schnitzel listens as more kids talk about what they did on Election Day, but Harry is thinking about Diamond's mom. He has been to Diamond's apartment. They even went out to dinner at Yummy Taco, both their families together.

When kids finish with their math sheets, they are allowed to draw until it's time for reading. Harry gets paper and folds it in half to make a card. He draws a chocolate cake on the cover, using brown crayon, and pink for candles. He isn't sure what to write inside.

Sorry you lost, he finally writes. He isn't sure he spelled it right, but he printed very neatly.

He pushes the card over to Diamond. "This is for your mom."

"She only likes vanilla cake," Diamond says, crumpling it up and shoving it in her backpack.

Harry feels himself flush. Why is Diamond so mean sometimes? She didn't even say the card was nice. She crumpled it!

Grrr. He feels like slamming his hands on the table, but he knows he shouldn't. What can he do?

"D and M," he finally says.

"What?" Diamond has been talking to Kimani as they transition to reading time.

Never mind. Harry doesn't want to explain. He picks a book and practices sounding out words, speaking softly to himself.

Silent *E* makes *cub* into *cube.*

It makes *fin* into *fine.*

He is going to remember that and not think about Diamond at all.

DAY 43. THURSDAY, NOVEMBER 8

This week's sight words are *first, again, because,* and *only.*

Everyone has to write sentences using the words to make a story. They don't have to worry about spelling, except for the sight words. Harry writes:

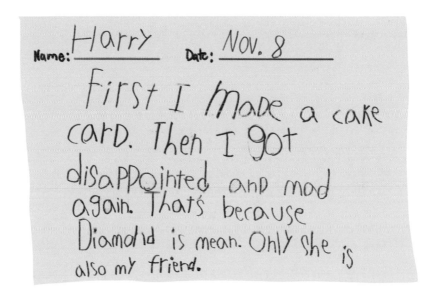

Name: Harry   Date: Nov. 8

First I made a cake card. Then I got disappointed and mad again. That's because Diamond is mean. Only she is also my friend.

Then he turns his paper over so Diamond won't see it.

When writing time is over, Diamond shows him *her* paper.

> Name: Diamond   Date: Nov.8
>
> First mom lost the election
> I was mean again to Harry.
> I was sad because I wished
> I wasn't mean. I wish I
> Was only nice all the
> time.

"My mom loved your card," she says. "She told me to say thank you."

"You're welcome."

Diamond smiles.

"I still think you're nice," says Harry.

"Okay, good," says Diamond. "I think you're nice, too."

Chapter 9
ABIGAIL

DAY 44. FRIDAY, NOVEMBER 9

During math, the students get to go to the gymnasium. Ms. Peek-Schnitzel has them line up in a row. Then they each take one hundred steps.

How surprising! They end up in different places. "Some people have longer strides," she explains. "One hundred is different for me than for you."

Abigail doesn't line up or step. She sits in a corner of the gym and puts her hands over her eyes.

Harry goes and sits by her. "Hi," he whispers.

"Mm," says Abigail.

"Watch me, okay?"

Abigail takes a hand off one eye.

Harry walks on tiptoe. He does it super funny.

Tippy-toe, tippy-toe! One hundred teeny tiny steps.

"Come on, Abigail!" he calls when he is finished. "I bet you can't take steps as small as me."

"Eyekendoo." Abigail answers so softly, Harry has to run back to hear her.

"What did you say?"

"I said, I can too."

Harry holds out his hand and Abigail takes it. He pulls her to standing.

Together they take the teeniest, tiniest tippy-toe steps, all the way to one hundred. Abigail's are even tinier than Harry's, but he doesn't mind.

Next they take one hundred *giant* steps.

And one hundred ballet leaps.

And one hundred T. rex leaps. Everyone joins in.

When they go back to class, Abigail is smiling.

Maybe I can be a stepping expert, thinks Harry. Or an Abigail expert.

But stepping isn't really something that needs experts. And Harry doesn't know if Abigail *really* lives with six dogs, so he's definitely not an Abigail expert yet.

He will have to keep working.

DAY 45. TUESDAY, NOVEMBER 13

There was no school on Monday. Harry spent the morning at Mason's, while Mommy was at work. Then Evaline picked him up, and Abigail came over to play. It was the first time she had been to Harry's apartment. She wanted to know the names of every single one of his stuffed animals. Evaline helped them bake chocolate chip cookies and Charlotte played Crazy Eights with them.

Today, Ms. Peek-Schnitzel writes the word *gratitude* on the Sparkly Word Wall. "Thanksgiving is coming up," she says. "At the Graham School, we study the history of that holiday in third and fourth grade. It is a complicated history to learn about, so in first grade, we mostly think about gratitude. That means feeling grateful and giving thanks."

Harry raises his hand. "*Thank you very much, you're welcome, please,* and *nice to meet you,*" he says. "Those are magic words my mom taught me."

Ms. Peek-Schnitzel smiles. "I like those words," she says, and writes *you're welcome* on the Sparkly Word Wall, too. "There is much to be thankful for," says Ms. Peek-Schnitzel, "but first, let's remember: not everyone sees Thanksgiving as a time for thanks. The holiday has to do with the arrival of Europeans to this land long ago. It was terrible in lots of ways for the Wampanoag, the Indigenous People who already lived in the Northeast, where the pilgrims landed. Many died and lost much of the land their people had always lived on. There is still sadness about that. Let's reflect."

They sit in silence for a moment. Harry looks at his hands. He didn't know there was a sad history to Thanksgiving.

"Thank you for thinking about that history with me," says the teacher. "Now, on a brighter note, what do you feel gratitude for?"

Diamond says ice cream.

Mason says Pebble.

Kimani says yarn.

"Why yarn?" asks the teacher.

"It makes me happy," says Kimani. "I can make things. And it comes in so many colors."

Wyatt says his grandma.

Abigail says she is grateful for Harry because he cheers her up when she is having a tough day.

Harry *was* going to say he feels grateful for Fluff Monsters, but he remembers Abigail, and the teeny tiny steps they did, and the playdate, and the Fluff Monster book from the library. "I am grateful for Abigail, too," he says.

DAY 46. WEDNESDAY, NOVEMBER 14

Harry *never* should have said he was grateful for Abigail. Now, at lunchtime, Wyatt goes:

Abigail and Harry

Sitting in a tree,

K-I-S-S-

I-N-G.

"Nuh-uh, Wyatt," says Abigail quietly.

But Wyatt says it again.

Diamond steps in, louder. "Leave them alone. You don't know what you're talking about."

Harry just eats his cold dumplings and says nothing. He doesn't want to get Wyatt mad in case Wyatt starts talking about pulling down pants.

Wyatt says the rhyme again.

"Stop it!" yells Diamond. "You're bothering them. And it's not even a good poem."

But Wyatt keeps going.

Abigail climbs under the cafeteria table.

Harry wants to make Wyatt stop, but no words will come out of his mouth.

DAY 47. THURSDAY, NOVEMBER 15

When Harry says hi to Abigail, Wyatt makes a kissy face.

When Harry hands Abigail a pencil, kissy face.

He even chants, quietly, during reading.

Abigail and Harry

Sitting in a tree,

K-I-S-S-

I-N-G!

First comes love,

Then comes marriage,

Then comes Harry with a baby carriage!

"Wyatt," says Ms. Peek-Schnitzel. "I am at the end of my patience with that rhyme. Would you please keep your opinions to yourself?"

"It's not an opinion," says Wyatt. "It's a true fact."

DAY 48. FRIDAY, NOVEMBER 16

Today Harry has a plan. He got advice from Charlotte last night. He just has to wait till lunchtime.

"Abigail and Harry, sitting in a tree," says Wyatt, as they all sit down with their pizza in the cafeteria.

"Nuh-uh," says Abigail again. Her eyes look big and watery.

"You're getting on my nerves, Wyatt," says Diamond.

But Wyatt doesn't stop.

Harry speaks loudly, saying the rhyme Charlotte taught him:

Happy llama, sad llama

Totally rad llama

Super llama, drama llama

Big fat mama llama!

Don't forget Obama llama, yes, we can!

Moose, alpaca!

Moose, moose, alpaca!

Moose, alpaca!

Moose, moose, alpaca!

He does the hand movements Charlotte taught him, making hand llamas that swoop and wiggle with his fingers.

"Ooh, what's that?" says Wyatt.

"Yeah, show us," says Diamond.

Everyone does "Happy Llama, Sad Llama" for the rest of lunch and recess.

Wyatt doesn't sing the "Sitting in a Tree" song again. He has forgotten all about it in the fun of "Moose, Moose, Alpaca."

Harry is grateful for the llama rhyme. And for Charlotte, too.

Chapter 10
POM-POMS

DAY 49. MONDAY. NOVEMBER 19

Today, Kimani's mom comes to school to teach the children how to make tiny pom-poms. She wears her hair in a printed kerchief and carries a huge bag of craft supplies.

Kimani looks so proud and happy.

Harry wishes his mom would come to the classroom to do crafts, too. Or his dad. If Daddy visited,

he could teach everyone that funny dance that's like a monkey.

Kimani's mom shows the kids how to wrap yarn around a plastic fork. You tie it in the middle and then cut the edges to take it off.

"Then you fluff it out," she says, holding up a pom-pom.

She has four different colors of yarn.

Harry makes green pom-poms. So does Diamond. Abigail makes purple. Mason and Wyatt make yellow.

Kimani starts with red but switches her yarn so her pom-poms have all different colors together. She is good at making them already. "I do it at home all the time," she tells the kids at Goat Table.

Then everyone glues their pom-poms to the ends of pipe cleaners so they look like flowers. They tie their bouquets with white lacy bows.

"White lacy bows are for girls," says Wyatt scornfully.

"People shouldn't limit themselves," says Kimani. "That's what my parents say."

DAY 50. TUESDAY, NOVEMBER 20

Jobs change again today.

Harry doesn't get to be Line Leader. Mia does.

Harry is only Electrician. He turns off the lights when the students leave the room.

The sight words for the week are *his, her, old,* and *stop.* As usual, Ms. Peek-Schnitzel wants the students to write four sentences to make a story using the words.

But today, Harry can't think of any sentences. His brain won't make them.

Wyatt is writing. Mason is writing. Kimani and Abigail and Diamond are writing.

Harry drums on the table.

Pom-pom (pause)

A dom-pom-pom

Pom-pom (pause)

A dom-pom-pom

"Harry, my friend?" says the teacher.
"Yes?"

"Please remember your sight words."

But Harry really feels like drumming. So he drums with sight words.

Old pom-pom

His pom-pom

Old pom-pom

Her pom-pom

Mason has written his sentences already, so now he starts drumming, too. Together they go:

Old pom-pom

His pom-pom

Her pop-pom

Stop!

Old pom-pom

His pom-pom

Her pom-pom

Stop!

"Hello again." Now the teacher is standing over them. "Mr. Mason and Mr. Harry, what is going on here? There's a lot of noise."

"I finished my sentences," says Mason.

Ms. Peek-Schnitzel looks at his paper. "Yes, you did," she says. "So I'm going to ask you to choose a book from the book bin. You may read until the lesson is over. Now, Harry?" Her voice is loud.

Harry puts his head down on the desk.

Ms. Peek-Schnitzel clears her throat. "Why is your head down?"

The words come out small. "You always yell at me."

"I do raise my voice sometimes when my students are not listening," she says, more gently.

Harry keeps his face down on the table. "It's still yelling."

"Well." Ms. Peek-Schnitzel takes a deep breath and exhales. "I don't want to be yelling. I really don't. But sometimes I feel frustrated, just the way you probably do."

"Harry made a poem, Ms. Peek-Schnitzel," says Diamond suddenly.

"Excuse me?" says the teacher.

"He made a poem from his sight words. He had to drum it to make the rhythm good."

The teacher wrinkles her brow, but she softens and says, "All right, Harry, would you say your poem for me?"

Harry sits up. He doesn't dare drum, again, so he says the rhythm by itself. His voice feels tiny. He stares down at the table as he speaks.

Old pom-pom
His pom-pom
Her pop-pom
Stop!
Old pom-pom
His pom-pom
Her pop-pom
Stop!

"That will do very nicely," says Ms. Peek-Schnitzel.

"It will?" Harry is surprised.

"It's got a great rhythm," says the teacher. "Now write it down, please. Silently."

DAY 51. WEDNESDAY, NOVEMBER 21

"What are you doing for the break?" the teacher asks at morning meeting. "I am going with Carl and my mother to Carl's brother's house for Thanksgiving. He is a terrible cook, so I always volunteer to bake the pies. Carl makes green bean casserole."

Kids raise their hands and say what their plans are. Wyatt's grandma is having people over. Wyatt will help make cranberry sauce. Diamond's mothers will have a party with rainbow tablecloths and not call it Thanksgiving at all. Abigail's family will volunteer at a homeless shelter in the morning. Then they'll have a cake with candles because it's Abigail's birthday.

Harry and Charlotte will visit their father in Boston. Mommy is renting a car and will drive them tonight. On the phone, their dad said he bought an apple pie for him and a chocolate cake for Harry and Charlotte. Daddy will make a chicken, since none of them likes turkey, and they'll have biscuits and gravy. They will watch the Thanksgiving Day parade on TV.

Harry doesn't know how to explain all this to the class, though, so he doesn't raise his hand until the teacher asks about gratitude again.

"I'm grateful for chocolate cake," he says.

Chapter 11
PUKE

DAY 52. MONDAY. NOVEMBER 26

When they come back after the break, it is Abigail's school birthday celebration. Her dad brings carrot cupcakes to the classroom after lunch.

Yuck.

Harry looks around the table. Diamond and Abigail are eating theirs happily. So are Mason, Kimani, and Wyatt.

Harry licks the frosting off his cupcake and leaves the cake part alone. It feels rotten to get excited about a cupcake and then for it not to be chocolate. Or even vanilla.

His tummy isn't happy. That frosting was kind of blechy.

Then Harry pukes. All across the desk. It comes out in one big blurp.

Diamond screams. Mason screams. Abigail and Kimani scream.

Wyatt laughs.

Everything is loud.

Ms. Peek-Schnitzel asks if he's okay.

No, he is not.

She wipes the puke from Harry's shirt and jeans. Even his shoes. Then she asks for a volunteer to take him to the nurse while she cleans up the table and the floor.

Mason takes him. He gives Harry his blue-and-red plastic horse to hold. "Ice Cream McGee will make you feel better," says Mason as he heads back to class. "He's a get-well horse."

DAY 53. TUESDAY, NOVEMBER 27

Harry does not go to school today. He stays home sick with the flu. He even has a temperature.

Mommy stays home with him. She reads the beginning of a chapter book about a bear who might be named Edward and might be named something else, but it's hard to understand and he keeps falling asleep, so she lets him play *Fluff Monsters* instead. He has to eat tummy medicine that tastes like chalk, but he still pukes three times.

DAY 54. WEDNESDAY, NOVEMBER 28

Harry does not go to school today, either, even though his temperature is almost normal.

He and his mother play Go Fish, War, and Crazy Eights. Mommy makes plain rice and Harry eats a little of it. They watch funny animal videos. They also read Harry's book from the library, the one about wild boars, four times.

Harry thinks the wild boars look like guinea pigs, but Mommy says they don't, at all.

When she gets home from school, Charlotte sits on his bed to do her homework. The two of them watch TV. Evaline calls to talk to him. So does Daddy. And he manages to eat some chicken and applesauce for dinner.

When he isn't puking, it really isn't that bad, being sick.

DAY 55. THURSDAY, NOVEMBER 29

Harry is back at school.

"Don't feel embarrassed," says Abigail, running up as soon as Harry walks into the classroom. "Everybody pukes."

"It's true." Kimani nods. "Puking is for everyone."

"I puked on the subway once," says Diamond.

"I puked at my aunt's house," says Mia.

"I puked on my mom," says Robbie.

"I puked once and it was pink," says Orlando. "Because I ate raspberries right before."

"I puked once and it had popcorn in it," says Mason. "Like big, puffy popcorn blobs. Plus the whole Halloween disaster."

"I never puked," says Wyatt.

"Not even when you were a baby?" asks Abigail.

"Well, sure, when I was a baby," says Wyatt. "But that doesn't count."

"I don't want to talk about puke!" cries Harry. "I'm sick and tired of puke."

Mason pats his arm. "It's so interesting to everyone," he says kindly. "We can't help it."

Chapter 12
GUINEA PIGS

DAY 56. FRIDAY, NOVEMBER 30

Harry and Charlotte are walking to school. "I have to tell you something," says Charlotte.

"What?"

"We have a class guinea pig now. In room 4-303."

"That's terrible!"

"No it's not. Her name is Goblin," says Charlotte. "You'll like her."

But Harry will not. He doesn't want to meet a guinea pig. Even in a cage.

He figures a guinea pig is a large pig with tusks and teeth. It will be all slobbery. It might snort at him with its big wet nose.

At morning meeting, Harry raises his hand. "Did

you know that there's a guinea pig in room 4-303?" he asks.

"Sure," says Ms. Peek-Schnitzel. "Goblin."

Kimani raises her hand. "I love guinea pigs."

Robbie raises his. "I love guinea pigs even more than Kimani does."

"You don't know that," snaps Kimani. "You can't measure love."

"I don't like them," says Harry.

"I thought everybody loved guinea pigs," says Robbie. "Like, everybody in the whole world."

Ms. Peek-Schnitzel decides to take a poll, the way they did with the apples in science class. She writes *Do you like guinea pigs?* on the whiteboard. Each kid says yes or no.

Twenty-three students like them.

Two students do not: Harry and Abigail.

"Now I feel weird for hating them," whispers Harry to Abigail.

"Not weird," says Abigail. "Unusual."

DAY 57. MONDAY, DECEMBER 3

Charlotte shows up at the door of Ms. Peek-Schnitzel's first-grade class. "Can Harry come to my classroom for a visit, to meet our guinea pig?" she asks the teacher.

Ms. Peek-Schnitzel tells Harry he may go, but Harry shrinks into himself and shakes his head.

"Don't you want to?" asks the teacher.

No. Harry already *told* Charlotte no. Why is she here talking about it again? He pulls his sweatshirt up to hide his face.

DAY 58. TUESDAY, DECEMBER 4

It is library day. Everyone climbs into the make-believe ship. Ms. Tellicherry reads a story about a tiger who stops wearing clothes and runs around naked. It is so funny!

When it is time to choose books, Ms. Peek-Schnitzel walks over to Harry. "I found a book about guinea pigs," she says, kneeling next to him. "A science book. Would you like to take it home?"

No way. Harry doesn't want that yucky book. Why is everyone always trying to push guinea pigs on him?

He's going to take the naked tiger book home, and that's all there is to it.

DAY 59. WEDNESDAY, DECEMBER 5

In science, Mr. Daryl is done with apples and pumpkins. Now he is teaching about sharks.

The children are supposed to copy the shark names into their science notebooks. Harry arranges his so they look like a poem and shows it to Diamond.

Nurse sharks, angel sharks,
Hammerheads and great whites.

Bramble sharks, carpet sharks,

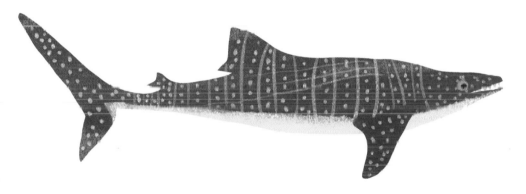

Cookie-cutter, lemon.

"I know you think I'm gonna say it's a poem," she says. "But it's not. Those are just shark names."

The sharks have all different shapes and sizes. Harry likes the cookie-cutter shark, because it sounds like cookies. And because of its triangle teeth.

As the class lines up, Mr. Daryl calls Harry up to his desk. "I heard you might need some information about guinea pigs," the teacher says.

"That's okay," says Harry. "I don't need to hear about them."

"Are you sure?"

"Yes, please," says Harry. "And thank you very much, you're welcome!"

DAY 60. THURSDAY, DECEMBER 6

Charlotte taps on the door of Harry's classroom just after morning meeting.

Really? Again?

Harry is not going up to fourth grade. He's just *not going.*

Ms. Peek-Schnitzel beckons Charlotte in, but Harry's sister disappears for a moment into the hallway. She comes back with another fourth grader. Together, they lug a wire cage that has wood shavings at the bottom.

"This isn't her regular cage," Charlotte says. "It's her travel cage."

Peeking out is a live Fluff Monster. For real!

It is fluffy like a Fluff Monster.

It has brown and white spots like a Fluff Monster might have.

It has cute beady eyes like a Fluff Monster, and stubby legs that are so short it looks like its feet are attached directly to its body.

It is the cutest thing in the world.

Charlotte and her friend set the cage right in front of Harry. The Fluff Monster wrinkles its nose and makes a snuffling sound. Harry reaches his finger out to stroke its fluffy head.

"I still don't like them," says Abigail.

"Don't like what?" says Harry.

"Guinea pigs," says Abigail.

"This is Goblin?" Harry can't believe it.

"This is Goblin," says Charlotte.

He keeps stroking Goblin gently on the head. Her fur is soft, and he can tell she's a little nervous. "I thought she was a giant scary pig," says Harry.

Charlotte laughs. "Really? But I told you you'd like her."

Ms. Peek-Schnitzel laughs, too. "I didn't know you thought *that,*" she says.

"She's a Fluff Monster," says Harry. "Look how cute." He pets Goblin again.

"Now that you say they're Fluff Monsters, I might have to start liking them," says Abigail.

DAY 61. FRIDAY, DECEMBER 7

Goblin is coming home with Harry and Charlotte. The guinea pig will live in her travel cage for the weekend. They can feed her and take her out, as long as it's just in the bathroom so she doesn't get lost.

But what does she eat? And how are you supposed to hold her?

During lunch, Harry goes upstairs to see Ms. Tellicherry in the library. She lets him return the naked tiger book and get the science book about guinea pigs.

Harry wants all the facts.

DAY 62. MONDAY, DECEMBER 10

Harry knows everything about guinea pigs now. Mommy read the science book to him, and they watched two videos about care and feeding. For example, he learned that guinea pigs mainly eat hay, but they need vitamin C, so broccoli and red pepper are very good for them. And they make a lot of noise, like chirping and purring.

After the videos, Harry and his mom looked at like, one hundred pictures of baby guinea pigs online. There are all different kinds! Ridgeback, Peruvian, Abyssinian, Silkie, and more. Goblin is an Alpaca guinea pig.

Harry and Charlotte carry Goblin back to school in her travel cage. Harry goes up to the fourth-grade classroom. It is full of seriously huge people.

Harry gets to transfer the guinea pig into her larger habitat. She feels quivery and warm in his hands.

He takes some cucumbers from his lunch box and puts them in her food bowl. "Bye-bye, Goblin. I love you. I'll come see you again soon." Then he turns to Charlotte's teacher, Ms. Gillooley. "Guinea pigs need friends," he tells her. "I learned it from my library book. Goblin needs at least one other guinea pig in order to be happy. Also, she likes strawberries, but she should only have them sometimes, for a treat."

"Thank you for telling me that, Harry," says Ms. Gillooley. "I will take that information very seriously."

"You're welcome," says Harry.

As he walks back downstairs to Ms. Peek-Schnitzel's first grade, Harry realizes something: it is the last thing he ever thought he'd be, but Harry Bergen-Murphy is now a guinea pig expert.

Chapter 13
FRIENDS

DAY 63. TUESDAY, DECEMBER 11

Today is the first day Ms. Peek-Schnitzel's kids have computer class. They will have computer once a week for ten weeks. Everyone is so excited. The computer teacher is Ms. DeRosa. She wears all black and has her hair in a

tight bun. She smiles at them as she wheels in one cart and then another, both filled with laptops.

"Everybody sit on your hands," she tells them.

All the kids sit on their hands while Ms. DeRosa puts a laptop in front of each person. Harry wants to touch his so badly! He is allowed to play on Mommy's tablet but never her computer.

Finally, they open their laptops. The teacher explains all the parts. Each computer has a screen, a keyboard, and a trackpad. "Please don't touch any buttons on the keyboard!" she says. "You are still just looking with your eyes."

Ms. DeRosa makes sure they all have a program open about honeybees. It's a game! Now she lets them use the trackpad. Harry practices using it to touch bees that are flying across the screen. Next, they practice dragging the bees down to flowers so they can go home to make honey.

Mason leans over. "It's not as good as *Fluff Monsters*," he says. "Plus I know how to use a trackpad already."

"It's almost as good," says Harry. "My bees are gonna make so much honey."

Later, the students do a keyboarding exercise. They have to find the letters of the alphabet and type them. *A* is for *anteater,* and when you have typed all your *A*s, an anteater pops up on the screen. *B* is for *bear.*

Harry is glad because after he types all his *G*s, there is a goat. And he sits at Goat Table!

He looks up to tell Mason, but Mason is sitting still, with his lower lip sticking out.

"What's wrong?" whispers Harry. Ms. DeRosa asked them to stay quiet.

"I got bored. Then I typed buttons I wasn't supposed to type," says Mason. "Or maybe I clicked something. I'm not sure." He turns the screen to face Harry. It has a bunch of words on it in a tiny font. "I can't make the animals come back. The computer went blurp!"

"Let's close it and hide it," says Harry. "Then she'll never know."

"Great idea," says Mason.

"She'll be able to tell," whispers Diamond, still typing. "She knows we are six kids at Goat Table, so there must be six computers."

"Mason can go to the bathroom," says Harry. "Then there will be only five kids."

"I'm going right now," Mason tells Harry. "You hide the computer."

Mason goes over to Ms. Peek-Schnitzel and gets the bathroom pass. Harry closes Mason's computer and slides it onto his lap.

Where can he hide it? Can he get it into one of the book bins? Will it fit in someone's backpack? Can he put it underneath a pillow in the reading area?

Oh, no! Ms. DeRosa is coming over to Goat Table. Harry shoves Mason's laptop up his shirt.

Then he goes back to typing. *H* is for *hippo*.

Ms. DeRosa looks at the screens for each kid. She squats down by Harry.

He is feeling kind of sweaty, but he keeps typing. *I* is for *iguana*. *J* is for *jaguar*.

"Excuse me," says the teacher. "I think one of my computers has climbed up your shirt."

"Oooh, busted," says Diamond, very quiet.

"Will you take it out, please?" says Ms. DeRosa. "That's not how we handle our laptops at the Graham School."

Mason comes back from the bathroom. He sees what is happening and stands frozen in the doorway. Harry takes the laptop out from under his shirt and gives it to the teacher.

"What is going on here?" Ms. DeRosa asks Goat Table.

No one says a word.

Ms. DeRosa looks at her clipboard. "I see this is computer number five and it was checked out to Mason. Which one of you is Mason?"

No one answers. Harry bites his lip.

Finally, Mason comes over. "I am Mason, and I typed keys I should not type," he says. "Sorry."

"I am Harry, and I put the laptop up my shirt," says Harry. "I'm sorry, too."

DAY 64. WEDNESDAY, DECEMBER 12

Ms. Peek-Schnitzel makes a chart of people's ages. It has numbers up to one hundred. She tells them her age. She is sixty-three years old. Her husband, Carl, is sixty-four. Her mother, Nanny, is ninety.

In Harry's home, Mommy is thirty-eight, Harry is five, and Charlotte is nine. All the kids chart the ages of the people who live with them.

Students want to include their dogs and cats and ferrets, but Ms. Peek-Schnitzel says it's only for humans. "Our chart shows one hundred years," she explains. "Humans can live to be one hundred, but dogs and cats never do."

"But they *could*," says Mason.

"No, sadly, they can't," says the teacher. "I'm sorry."

"But *maybe*," says Mason.

"It isn't going to happen, I'm afraid," says the teacher. "I wish it were different, though."

"We don't know for sure," says Mason. "It still could maybe happen."

"We're only going to put people on the chart," says Ms. Peek-Schnitzel.

"I don't want Pebble to die," says Mason.

DAY 65. THURSDAY, DECEMBER 13

Harry's wiggly tooth falls out during morning meeting. Just falls out! He feels it in his mouth and then it is in his hand, looking small and a bit bloody.

The teacher helps him save it in a plastic baggie. He shows everybody the gap in his mouth. It feels slippery when he touches it with his tongue.

"You have a real first grader smile now," says Ms. Peek-Schnitzel. "You must be getting comfortable in first grade. Am I right?"

She *is* right. Harry grins.

At recess, Harry and Mason sit side by side on top of the small climbing structure. "I don't want to turn six," Mason says.

"Why not?" Harry asks. "I want to turn six."

"I just don't."

"But you have your party. I'm going to your party," Harry says. Mason's party is coming up.

"I want my party," says Mason. "I just don't want to get old. What did it feel like to lose your tooth?"

"It felt unusual," says Harry.

DAY 66. FRIDAY, DECEMBER 14

All morning, Mason keeps poking his teeth and telling Harry they are wiggly, but Harry isn't so sure. During writing, the students have to write four sentences using their sight words of the week: *friend, tired, play,* and *happy.*

Mason writes:

Name: Mason   Date: Dec.14

My friend was a dog.
She got tired and died.
We cannot play.
I will never be happy.

Harry is still trying to think of sentences. He looks at Mason's paper. "Did Pebble die?" he asks.

"No," says Mason. "It's just a story."

"Why did you write a sad story?"

"My babysitter's dog died," says Mason. "So now I'm worried."

Harry looks at Mason. Then he writes his own story.

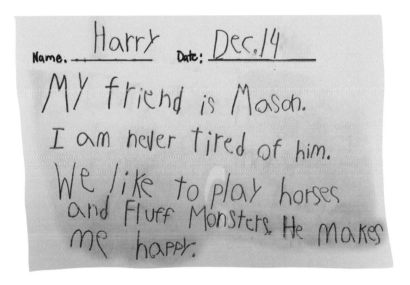

Name. __Harry__ Date: __Dec.14__

MY friend is Mason.
I am never tired of him.
We like to play horses
and Fluff Monsters. He makes
me happy.

He reads it to Mason. Mason grins. "'Cause we're best friends, right?" he says.

"Right," says Harry.

"You guys are always talking about what best friends you are," says Diamond.

"Yup!" says Harry.

"But you know," says Diamond, "you could have lots of best friends. It doesn't have to be leaving other kids out, the way you make it."

"What?" Harry never thought of it like that.

"It's true," says Kimani. "You talk about it *a lot*. Like, I could say I have a first best friend and a second best friend and a third best friend. I could say that, and give people numbers, but I don't. Because it could make kids cry and stuff, that's why. And my parents said not to."

Oh.

Harry looks at Abigail. She has finished her sentences and is tracing her name over and over with a pink pencil.

He looks at Wyatt. Wyatt is done writing and now has a book to practice reading. Neither of them glances up.

Harry feels himself flush. He is glad when Ms. Peek-Schnitzel asks them to get in line for lunch.

Chapter 14
WINTER HOLIDAYS

DAY 67. MONDAY, DECEMBER 17

Winter break is coming soon. Kids are talking about baking Christmas cookies and going to see the decorated windows of the department stores. Kimani is making people presents out of yarn. Harry and Mason went ice skating on Saturday with Harry's mom. Abigail and Diamond saw *The Nutcracker*.

Some people are going on trips while school is out, but Harry will stay home. Baba and Grandpa Mike will come to visit and sleep in the living room. They will make latkes for Hanukkah. Harry and Charlotte will get presents. On Christmas Day, the family will go out for Chinese food and a movie. Harry won't see his dad, because Daddy is going to Ireland.

At morning meeting, Ms. Peek-Schnitzel writes the

word *tradition* on the Sparkly Word Wall. She explains that it means a thing your family does every year, passed on from grandparents to parents to kids. "What winter holiday do you celebrate?" she asks.

Everyone raises a hand.

"Let's make a list," says Ms. Peek-Schnitzel. "Our traditions might be different, but we all have them. We might eat special foods, or pray, or do ceremonies, see family, or have parties." Kids all want to share their traditions. Some students celebrate just one holiday. Some celebrate more than one. The teacher writes on the whiteboard.

"It's a poem!" shouts Diamond after everyone has spoken.

And so it is.

They practice saying the list together.

Christmas. Christmas.
Kwanzaa and Christmas.
Hanukkah. Hanukkah. Hanukkah and Christmas.

Solstice. Hanukkah. Christmas. Christmas.

Christmas. Diwali, but it's over already.

Ramadan, but it's not yet.

(and pause)

Ramadan, but it's not yet.

(and pause)

Christmas. Christmas.

Kwanzaa and Christmas.

New Years!

Hanukkah. Nikommo, and Christmas.

Bodhi Day. Hanukkah. Christmas. Christmas.

Christmas and Diwali, but it's already done!

Harry starts clapping out the rhythm as they read it.

The other kids clap, too. It is such a happy beat.

"Can we do it again?" he asks when they have finished. Ms. Peek-Schnitzel invites everyone to stand. She points at the words as they clap and dance to the rhythm of their first-grade holiday poem.

DAY 68. TUESDAY, DECEMBER 18

It's Holiday Feast Day in Ms. Peek-Schnitzel's class. Parents and caregivers come in the morning and bring snacks to celebrate the season. Harry's mom is here.

They are not harvest snacks, thank goodness. Instead, there are round pecan cookies dusted with powdered sugar, carrot cupcakes from Abigail's dad, candied orange peel, and thin Russian pancakes. Also, brownies with red and green candy on top, cinnamon buns, baklava, and tiny cupcakes, decorated blue and white for Hanukkah.

Some parents explain how the food they brought connects to their family traditions, but honestly, Harry doesn't listen. He is too busy eating brownies.

Everyone fills their plates, and the classroom is buzzy and happy.

Then Wyatt pukes. He pukes all across Goat Table.

And the floor.

And the chair.

And his shoes.

Diamond screams. Mason screams. Harry's plate of treats is all pukey. Ms. Peek-Schnitzel runs over with a towel and begins wiping Wyatt.

"It is too much sugar," says Wyatt's grandma, touching his back.

Wyatt is crying. Big blobby tears run down his face and into his drool and into his puke. Grown-ups run around with damp paper towels, helping to clean. Kids scream and point.

Harry is sad about his plate of treats, but he remembers how it felt to puke at school.

Terrible, that's how.

Poor Wyatt.

Harry goes to the classroom sink. He gets a paper towel and wets it. He gives it to Wyatt so Wyatt can wipe his face. "I'll take him to the bathroom," Harry tells Wyatt's grandma.

He gets the bag of extra clothes from Wyatt's cubby and they go together down the hall.

DAY 69. WEDNESDAY, DECEMBER 19

Wyatt is back at school already. "Careful with your pants!" he says to Harry as he slides into his chair for math. Wyatt reaches over and pulls back Harry's waistband. Snap!

"Wyatt!" The name pops out of Harry's mouth, pretty loud.

"What?" says Wyatt. "I'm just kidding."

"Stop it." Harry can't quite believe how strong and bossy his own voice sounds.

"What's the big whup?" says Wyatt. "It's a joke."

Harry thinks about what Ms. Peek-Schnitzel has told him about using his words to say his feelings. "Stop it. Stop it forever, please, because it scares me. And thank you very much."

"Stop it from me, too," says Diamond. "That isn't how you tell a joke, Wyatt."

"Me too," says Mason. "Stop it forever and ever."

"Whatever." Wyatt looks at his five table mates. Then he looks away. Ms. Peek-Schnitzel puts a bin of Math-link cubes on Goat Table. Wyatt gets very interested in choosing red and yellow cubes. They all get interested in choosing cubes.

"Okay, fine, I'll stop it," says Wyatt finally.

DAY 70. THURSDAY, DECEMBER 20

During art, Ms. Yoo sets out jars of craft supplies. "We're going to make holiday picture frames for your families," she says. "You'll cover a cardboard frame with buttons, pasta, beans, and other items. When the frame is all decorated, bring it to me and I'll spray-paint it gold or silver. It'll be ready to take home tomorrow, once it's dry."

There are six shapes of pasta, several kinds of dried beans, buttons in different sizes, paper clips, Legos, and more. Students each get a bowl. They walk around collecting what they want to glue onto their picture frames.

Harry starts with bow-tie pasta. He glues them across the bottom of his frame and up one side, but when he goes back to get more, they're gone. No more bow ties.

Wyatt has a different problem. He started with sequins, and they're so tiny, they're hard to work with. He only has one line of them along the edge.

"I'll never finish," he says.

"*I'll* never finish," says Harry.

"What if I get you more bow ties and you can help me glue sequins?" Wyatt suggests.

Harry isn't sure he wants to work with Wyatt.

"I know Amira and Robbie both have bow ties," coaxes Wyatt. "I can definitely get you more."

Okay, then. Wyatt gets Amira and Robbie to share

their bow ties while Harry glues sequins on Wyatt's picture frame.

"My grandma is going to be happy," says Wyatt when the projects are done.

"My baba is going hug it and kiss it and carry it in her purse all the time," says Harry.

Ms. Yoo spray-paints both picture frames a beautiful gold.

DAY 71. FRIDAY, DECEMBER 21

On the day before winter break, the Graham School hosts a holiday concert during last period. The music teacher, Ms. Boggs, stands up and gives a speech. Ms. Peek-Schnitzel's kids stand with the other first-grade classes and sing "Jingle Bell Rock." They all have jingle bells to shake during the song.

After the concert, there is a bustle of coats and hats. Grown-ups say "Have a good holiday" and "Happy new year."

Everyone walks out of the auditorium into the snow.

It falls joyfully on Harry's face as he holds hands with Mommy and Evaline. Charlotte walks ahead with a group of her friends.

"Hey, Harry!" Wyatt calls. He is with his grand-mother, just behind them.

Harry turns around.

Bam! A snowball hits him in the arm. Snowball fight!

"I'll get you!" Harry yells, bending down to scoop some snow into a ball. He throws it at Wyatt.

Thwack! It hits Wyatt on the leg.

Wyatt makes one and throws it back. It hits Harry's shoulder and sprays snow onto his mom.

"Kids," says Mommy, laughing. "Please."

Wyatt throws another. Harry throws another.

Wyatt throws one that goes right in Harry's face.

"Children," scolds Wyatt's grandma. "That's enough. You're getting snow on everyone."

Then they're at the corner. Harry has to turn, head-ing down the street to his apartment. Wyatt and his grown-ups begin to cross the street.

"Woo-hoo!" yells Wyatt. "I got you with that last one, didn't I?"

"Yup, you did," yells Harry. "But I'll get you next time!"

Wyatt laughs. He's on the other side of the street now.

"Bye, Wyatt," calls Harry. "See you next year!"

Chapter 15
COMMUNITY WORKERS

DAY 72. WEDNESDAY, JANUARY 2

Harry didn't think he'd want to go back to school after vacation, but he feels fizzy as he steps into the classroom.

He saw Diamond and Mason for playdates over the break, and he went to Mason's birthday party, but now, here is Ms. Peek-Schnitzel in her gray old-lady cardigan, looking cozy and lipsticky like always. And here is Kimani, wearing a new sweater with a sequined cat on it. And here is Wyatt, with a purple Fluff Monster key chain dangling from his backpack.

"You like Fluff Monsters now?" Harry asks as they hang up their coats.

"Yup. I used to think they were baby stuff, but then I

got the game for Christmas," Wyatt says. "They're pretty boss. Hey, listen, what does a sick dog say?"

Harry thinks. "Help me, I have a tummy ache?"

"No, doof. It's a joke," says Wyatt.

"Oh. Does it say . . ." Harry pauses. He can't think of anything.

"It says *arf, arf,*" says Wyatt.

"What?" Harry doesn't get the joke.

"*Arf, arf* is not the answer," says Kimani, coming over to hang up her coat. "It's *barf, barf.* That's what a sick dog says. Get it?"

Barf, barf! "That's so funny!" says Harry.

"Oh, stupid," says Wyatt. "I forgot the thing it says. I can't believe I did that."

"I got a giant squid for Christmas," says Abigail, coming to the cubby area. "I was worried it would eat my six dogs, but it turns out squids don't eat dogs. Squiddy eats watermelon."

Harry isn't sure whether to believe her, so he just tells her about the set of toy horses he got from his dad.

DAY 73. THURSDAY, JANUARY 3

During lunch, Wyatt has another joke. "What did one booger say to the other?"

"I know that one," says Kimani. "My brothers do gross jokes all the time."

"Don't tell!" cries Wyatt.

"Did it say, 'You're so yucky'?" asks Mason.

"Nope."

"Did it say, 'Let's live in this nose together'?" asks Harry.

"No way."

"Okay," says Harry. "What did the booger say?"

"It said, you think you're funny," says Wyatt.

Huh? Harry doesn't get it.

"The right answer is 'You think you're funny, but you're SNOT,'" says Kimani.

"Snot!" Snot always makes Harry laugh. It is so disgusting!

Mason laughs, too.

Wyatt looks down at his hands. "Snot," he repeats to

himself, like he's practicing. "But you're SNOT. I have to remember *but you're SNOT.*"

DAY 74. FRIDAY, JANUARY 4

Ms. Peek-Schnitzel teaches them the song "Who Are the People in Your Neighborhood?" Kids get to call out different community workers.

"Nurse," says Harry, because that's what Mommy is.

"Mechanic," says Wyatt.

"Fire chief," says Kimani.

"Subway driver," says Diamond.

"Dog walker," says Mason.

"Teacher," says Isabella.

"Squid," says Abigail.

The teacher stops for a moment. "Did you say *squid*?"

"Uh-huh. Squid," says Abigail.

"Well, we're getting silly now, but sure," says Ms. Peek-Schnitzel. They all sing, "A squid is a person in your neighborhood!"

Harry wonders about Abigail's giant squid. Does it live in a fish tank? Can it do any tricks? What does it eat besides watermelon, and how giant is giant?

DAY 75. MONDAY, JANUARY 7

Today people get new classroom jobs. Harry is Book Bin Monitor.

It is an un-special job.

Also, Harry's dad was supposed to be in town over

the weekend, but he didn't come because of a problem at work. That was another un-special thing.

All day, nothing feels right. Harry struggles during reading. Ms. Peek-Schnitzel has moved him to a higher level of book, and that's good because he was tired of the stories in the old book bin, but it's also bad because the new books are hard. There are *CH* sounds and *SH* sounds and even more silent *E*s than before.

The books aren't making any sense, and the pictures aren't helping. Harry wants to smush his face onto the table and close his eyes.

At lunch, he feels like kicking chairs when Kimani gives Mason, and only Mason, a cookie from her lunch box. And during writing, he wants to slam his hands on the table when Diamond hogs the green pencil again.

Harry doesn't smush. Or kick. Or slam. But the bad feelings sit inside him all day.

"How come you're so grumpy?" asks Charlotte as they wait for Evaline in the yard. Evaline has come to pick them up, but she is making them wait while she rummages in her purse.

"It's nothing," says Harry.

"I think it's something," says Charlotte.

But still, Harry doesn't have words. He stomps his foot. Then he stomps his other foot. Then he stomps both his feet really fast, to let some of the grump out.

Charlotte bends over. "What's wrong, H?"

He stomps some more. "I miss Daddy," he says at last.

Charlotte takes his hand. They follow Evaline out of the yard. "I was super mad when he didn't come after school on Friday," says Charlotte. "I hate it when he does stuff like that."

"I love Daddy," says Harry loyally. Now that Charlotte is criticizing, he doesn't want to hear it.

"I love him, too," says Charlotte, "but he's not like, a dad you can count on for stuff. Perdita's dad lives far away, but you know what? He calls her every single Wednesday night. And he comes to visit every other weekend."

Harry nods. It would be nice to know when Daddy was going to call and visit. "D and M," he says to Charlotte.

"Yeah, D and M," she says.

Charlotte asks Evaline if she can go the bodega, which is the shop on the corner that sells snacks, groceries, and deli sandwiches. She runs inside while Harry and Evaline wait. When she comes out, she gives Harry a package of small chocolate cupcakes with fluffy frosting inside.

"You're special to me," Charlotte tells him.

DAY 76. TUESDAY, JANUARY 8

"Our class is learning about community by having grown-ups who are community workers come to school," says Ms. Peek-Schnitzel. "And today, we have four family members visiting."

Harry's mom is here. She sits in a chair during morning meeting and talks about her job as an intensive care nurse. "When people are really, really sick, or if they have had a bad accident," she says, "they stay in the intensive care part of the hospital. I see the very sickest people and help take care of them."

She wears her scrubs so the children can see her work uniform.

Diamond puts her hand up. "Do you do stitches?"

"No. But I keep the patients' wounds clean."

"How did you learn how?" asks Diamond.

"I went to nursing school."

"I didn't know there was school for stuff like that," says Diamond. "I thought it was just reading, math, and writing."

"There's school for nurses, artists, news reporters, electricians, all kinds of things," says Harry's mom.

When she is done, she sits next to Harry on the rug, just like a kid.

Wyatt's grandma is next. She runs the office for a garage where auto mechanics work. She explains how the garage fixes cars. It also has a car wash.

Kimani's dad is a fire chief. He brings a toy fire truck and explains all the parts and what they do.

Last is Abigail's mom. She runs an animal rescue center. They take care of dogs and cats who are lost or homeless. She shows the kids pictures on the SMART Board.

Elijah puts a hand up. "Do you have ferrets?"

"Sometimes. And sometimes birds and hamsters—but mostly cats and dogs," says Abigail's mom.

"Do you really have six dogs at home?" asks Harry.

"Yes. They are dogs who couldn't get adopted. It's a good thing we have a backyard."

"What about a giant squid?" asks Harry. "Abigail said you have a giant squid."

"The giant squid is a stuffed animal," says Abigail's mom. "But we treat it like family."

DAY 77. WEDNESDAY, JANUARY 9

"Your dad is so boss," says Harry to Kimani during lunch.

"Yup," says Kimani.

"My dad is just a manager," says Mason.

"My dad is just a veterinarian," says Abigail.

"Your dad is a veterinarian?" shrieks Harry. "That's even better than your mom being an animal rescue lady!"

Everyone wants to hear about being a vet. They all agree that when they grow up, they want to be vets, too.

Or maybe fire chiefs, like Kimani's dad.

Fire chief vets!

Wyatt doesn't say anything. He isn't eating, even though he has two Oreos in his lunch.

Mason, Kimani, and Abigail are all talking happily about the awesome dads.

Harry taps Wyatt on the shoulder. "Hey, my dad doesn't live with me," he says. "Did you know that? I wish he lived with me, but my parents got divorced."

"I don't have a dad at all," adds Diamond, "and both my moms have boring jobs."

"I only have a mom," says Wyatt.

"It's all good," says Diamond.

"How come you live with your grandma?" asks Harry.

"My mom is far away."

"Do you get to see her?" asks Harry.

"Sometimes." says Wyatt. "She's sick."

Harry doesn't know what to say. No one else seems to, either. Finally he says, "Your grandma is super cool. Do you get to visit the garage?"

Wyatt nods.

"Do you get to look at engines?"

"Yup, sometimes." Wyatt tells them about riding through the car wash, and looking in the toolboxes, and how the cars get jacked up so the repair people can go underneath them. "I'm the only kid mechanic they have there," he says proudly.

DAY 78. THURSDAY, JANUARY 10

Ms. Yoo has felt. Tons and tons of felt. "We're making shark heads," she announces. "I know you're studying sharks with Mr. Daryl."

She gives everyone scissors and shows them how to cut out the head shape. "Choose any color you want."

Harry makes a green shark.

Next, Ms. Yoo shows how to do the teeth and eyes.

Harry adds extra teeth.

At the end, they glue their shark heads to blue paper

that's supposed to be water. If they want, they can draw some little fish swimming around.

Harry adds fish. Abigail adds a giant squid. "You should come meet Squiddy and my dogs," says Abigail shyly. "I've been to your house already."

"Okay," says Harry.

"You could even come today if you want," says Abigail. "I think you can, I mean."

And Harry does. Evaline promises to pick him up at five, and he leaves the schoolyard with Abigail's mom.

Abigail's family lives in a town house, a narrow three-story building with a backyard and the kitchen on the second floor. Abigail introduces Harry to the six dogs and then to Squiddy and the other stuffed animals who live on her bed. Her room is painted dark pink. They go to the kitchen for graham bunnies and milk, and after that, they play dress-up and build a fort. Harry wears Abigail's chef costume and Abigail wears her doctor costume. All the stuffed animals are sick in the fort hospital, and Harry brings them good things to eat.

Squiddy eats toy watermelon.

Harry doesn't want to leave when Evaline comes to get him.

DAY 79. FRIDAY, JANUARY 11

During reading, something clicks. Silent *E* makes *glob* into *globe*. It turns *twin* into *twine*. Suddenly, it just makes sense.

Harry no longer has to stop at every word, check to see whether it has an *E* at the end, and then figure out what the sound in the middle might be. He just knows!

He raises his hand. Ms. Peek-Schnitzel comes over.

"Can I read some of my book to you?" asks Harry.

"Sure." She squats down to hear him and see the pictures.

It is a story about a mule who waves while she bakes a cake. Then she waves while she plays a game and waves while she rides a plane. Harry can read it without pausing.

After school, Daddy is waiting in the yard. He has

come for the weekend. He will stay at his friend Declan's place, the way he always does. Surprise!

Harry feels the grump he's been holding all week fade away. He loves Daddy and Daddy loves him. He knows it is true. He gives his dad the felt shark he made, which was dry enough to take home. Daddy promises to put it up on the wall of his apartment.

"How you been, H?" he asks, swinging Harry around while they wait for Charlotte to come out.

"I have lots of friends," says Harry. "There's Mason, Abigail, Diamond, and Kimani. And even Wyatt. Plus I can make a shark and a pom-pom. I can read words with silent *E* and I can count to one hundred."

"You can?" says Daddy.

"I can," says Harry.

With Charlotte, they take a train to Manhattan and go to Daddy's favorite pizza restaurant, the one with the giant melty wax candles. Afterward, they go to a nighttime superhero movie and take the subway back to Brooklyn.

Harry falls asleep on Daddy's shoulder as the train shuttles through the night.

Chapter 16
CHARLOTTE

DAY 80. MONDAY, JANUARY 14

Evaline has bags of cheese puffs for Harry and Charlotte when she picks them up. "We have to do some errands for your mother," she says cheerfully, "so I thought these might make the chores go faster."

It is icy cold on the street, but Harry and Charlotte take off their mittens and count the cheese puffs as they eat and walk. There are twenty-eight puffs in each bag.

In the steamy heat of the drugstore, they can look around while Evaline collects the things on her list. Harry wants to go to the toy aisle, to see if Evaline will get him anything. "Come on," he says, pulling Charlotte's hand. "Let's see if they have those bags of tiny plastic dinosaurs."

They are heading over when suddenly, Charlotte ducks into the boring shampoo aisle.

"Why are you stopping?"

"Perdita is over there," whispers Charlotte. "I don't want to see her."

"Your friend Perdita?"

"Yeah. But I'm D and M at her."

"How come?"

"She's not letting me play with her at recess."

"Why?" Harry wants to go to the toy aisle.

"She started up some game where she's a queen and Hannah's a court jester and some other people are royal pets, but they say I can only play if I'm the scullery maid," says Charlotte. "I don't want to be the scullery maid."

"What's a scullery maid?"

"I don't really know, but it's like scrubbing and taking out garbage and stuff, basically."

"Yuck. Royal pet is way better than scullery maid."

"Exactly."

Harry takes Charlotte's hand. He doesn't pull her to the toy aisle. They hold hands as they wait for Evaline to pay for things. They keep holding while Evaline picks up a bag of laundry at the Laundromat. They hold hands all the way home.

DAY 81. TUESDAY, JANUARY 15

Map time! All the kids have to draw maps of their bedrooms. "If you were up high, looking down at your bedroom from the ceiling, what would it look like?" asks Ms. Peek-Schnitzel. She shows them some examples.

Harry shares a room with Charlotte. They have twin beds. His bed has dinosaurs on the comforter. Her bed has lemons. It takes him a long time to draw the map because their room is messy. It's hard to show all the things that are piled up around, like stacks of books that aren't in the bookshelf and the stuffed animals that live in a laundry basket.

When he's done, Harry asks Ms. Peek-Schnitzel if he can take his map home.

"I was planning to hang them on the wall of our classroom," she says.

"I want to give it to my sister because she has a mean friend," says Harry.

The teacher says yes. Harry writes *For Charlotte* in big letters at the top of his map.

When he gives it to her after school, Charlotte tapes it to the door of their bedroom, where anyone walking down the hall can see it.

In science, Mr. Daryl has started teaching about weather, and in art, Ms. Yoo has them all make winter scenes. She shows them examples of how different artists have painted wind and snow. She says artists don't have to use white for snow. They might use yellow, purple, blue, or green, any color.

Harry wants to use white anyway. He takes blue paper and makes a small white snowman. Then he gets a big brush and makes a swirling, whirling snowstorm. It covers the snowman completely. Ms. Yoo hands out glitter. Silver glitter, gold glitter, blue and purple glitter, and glitter that's see-though and rainbow.

By the end of art, Harry has glitter all over him. In his ears, between his fingers, on his neck, on his clothes. So do the other kids at Goat Table.

"We look silly," says Wyatt sadly.

"Nuh-uh. We look boss," says Kimani.

"I think so, too," says Abigail. "We're sparkly."

"It shows we're artists," says Harry. "Like, everyone will know we did art today."

"We're a team of glitter people," says Mason.

"Yeah!" says Harry. "Team Glitter Goat. Okay?"

"Okay," agrees Wyatt.

"Team Glitter Goat is the greatest!" says Harry. "We'll be sparkly all over Brooklyn."

DAY 83. THURSDAY, JANUARY 17

During story time, Ms. Peek-Schnitzel reads aloud about Dr. Martin Luther King. He was like, the greatest community worker, the most awesome change maker, and the most important Line Leader of all.

The book explains how Dr. King made a big difference for Black people and their rights, and how he showed white people that they needed to work to make a difference, too. He changed the rules through peaceful actions. For example, now there are laws that say you can't separate people because of their color, and you can't be unfair to them because of their race, religion, gender, or background.

"This book reminds me that I need to speak up

against things that are wrong even when other people don't agree with me," says Ms. Peek-Schnitzel.

She writes the word *peaceful* up on the Sparkly Word Wall. "Dr. King taught me that I can be brave and fight for what's right and be peaceful at the same time." She adds, "We have Monday off to celebrate Dr. King's birthday."

Walking home with Charlotte and Evaline, Harry asks about Perdita. "Did you guys play today?"

"No," says Charlotte. "I played with Rosie and her friends. But it wasn't that fun."

"Are you gonna be the scullery maid tomorrow?" asks Harry.

"I don't think so," says Charlotte. "Not if she's the queen. If she wanted to be scullery maids together, that would be different."

DAY 84. FRIDAY, JANUARY 18

At the end of the school day, the class has a birthday party for Dr. King. Even though his real birthday was

January 15, today is the day before the holiday, so today is the day for cake. Ms. Peek-Schnitzel baked cupcakes— and yay! They are chocolate.

Together the students sing "Happy birthday, dear Martin."

Ms. Peek-Schnitzel shows part of a video of Dr. King's most famous speech, where he says, "I have a dream today!" He says he dreams that his "children will one day live in a nation where they will not be judged by the color of their skin, but by the content of their character."

"We can all be change makers," says the teacher. "And change making starts with having a dream." She asks the students to share their dreams for a better future.

"I dream all dogs have a home," says Abigail.

"Me too," says Mason.

"I dream that everyone votes, 'cause lots of people don't right now," says Diamond. "That's what my mom told me."

"I dream it doesn't matter who you love, 'cause love is love," says Orlando.

"I dream everybody recycles," says Jayden.

"I dream what Dr. King said about not judging other people," says Kimani.

Harry isn't sure what to dream. He wishes for all the things people have said. They're good things.

Finally, he puts his hand up. "I dream everyone speaks up when something's wrong," he says. "They use their words."

"I dream Spider-Man is real," says Wyatt.

"Me too," says Robbie.

"Let's be serious, please," says Ms. Peek-Schnitzel.

"I am serious," says Wyatt. "Spider-Man saves a lot of people. I wish he was real, so much."

DAY 85. TUESDAY, JANUARY 22

Part of social studies has been learning about garbage and waste. "Being responsible for our trash is an important element of being a good community member, because garbage hurts our oceans and our air," says Ms. Peek-Schnitzel.

The kids have learned the "three Rs" of talking about waste. The words are on the Sparkly Word Wall.

Reduce means to use less.

Reuse means to find new ways to use old items so that they don't go in the trash.

Recycle means to put certain things into bins so they can be made into new things.

Today they are reusing. This morning, kids brought in cereal boxes, paper-towel rolls, plastic take-out containers, used wrapping paper, packaging peanuts, milk cartons, and anything else they had around the house that could be reused. Harry brought in two shoe boxes and a tall, round oatmeal box.

Ms. Peek-Schnitzel brings out a huge piece of cardboard they will use as a base. "We will build a sculpture map of Gardener Street," she says. "We will be reusing all those items you brought from home."

She has a sketch that shows the locations of all the important buildings they've seen on their neighborhood walks. Each kid gets something to make. Wyatt has the fried chicken restaurant. Abigail is in charge of trees: ginkgoes, northern red oaks, and crabapples. Diamond has the toy store. Mason has D'Angelo's bakery. Kimani has the firehouse. Harry has the bodega.

Ms. Peek-Schnitzel ignores the usual afternoon schedule. The students work on the sculpture map, pasting, painting, and collaging. Ms. Yoo peeks in to see how it's going.

"Oh, I love this project!" she cries, her eyes shining.

Harry runs over to show Ms. Yoo how he covered a milk carton with yellow and red tissue and then drew windows with a black pen. "I'm going to put things in my windows, because you can really see things in the windows of the bodega," he tells Ms. Yoo.

"What are you going to put?" she asks.

"Chocolate cupcakes and cheese puffs," he says.

When he is finished, his milk carton looks just like the bodega. Harry writes *Deli-Grocery* on it, which is what it says on the real store's sign. He uses his neatest writing.

DAY 86. WEDNESDAY, JANUARY 23

During science, Mr. Daryl shows the kids some close-up photographs of snowflakes.

Wow.

They are like art. Harry has never seen anything as beautiful as real, live snowflakes.

The snow that lines the sidewalks in Brooklyn is icy and dirty, though. It's old snow, Harry thinks. The beauty is in *new* snow.

Wednesday is Harry and Charlotte's usual night to go to the dumpling restaurant for dinner. The family orders pork, vegetable, and shrimp dumplings.

"I don't want to be friends with Perdita anymore," says Charlotte. "She isn't nice to me."

"She used to be nice to you," says Harry.

"Yeah," says Charlotte. "But not anymore."

"Too much mean and not enough nice to mix in with it," says Mommy. "That's when it's okay to say goodbye."

Charlotte doesn't usually sit in her mother's lap. It's Harry's spot most of the time. But today, Charlotte finishes her dumplings and climbs on. Mommy eats with one hand, her other arm around Charlotte's shoulders.

As the three of them walk home, new snow begins to fall. Harry tells Mommy and Charlotte about the snowflake photographs. They look up to see the snow swirling in the light from the streetlamps. It looks like glitter.

Chapter 17
ONE HUNDRED SOMETHINGS

DAY 87. THURSDAY, JANUARY 24

"For our Hundred Days celebration, we will each bring in one hundred of something," Ms. Peek-Schnitzel reminds the class at morning meeting. "I will send a note home so your grown-ups know."

Mason raises his hand. "Can I bring one hundred boogers?" he asks.

"What do you think?" says the teacher.

"Boogers are all-natural," Mason says. "They come from your body, so nobody should be ashamed of them. That's what my dad says."

"It's true," Kimani adds. "Everybody has them."

"Hey," says Wyatt. "I have a booger joke. Can I tell it?"

"Let's not do boogers," says Ms. Peek-Schnitzel.

Harry puts his hand up. "Also, if you cut a booger up, you get more boogers."

Mason calls out. "Also, you could stick them together. If you stick them together, you get a giant booger."

Ms. Peek-Schnitzel doesn't call on anyone after that.

DAY 88. FRIDAY, JANUARY 25

Harry doesn't know what to bring for the one-hundredth day. Last night, his mom suggested Band-Aids.

But Band-Aids are boring.

On the phone, his dad suggested nails.

But nails are boring.

Charlotte told him to bring marshmallows. "That's the most popular thing to bring. Everyone loved Hannah when she brought marshmallows because they got to eat them at the end of the day."

But Wyatt is bringing marshmallows. Harry knows.

He mulls it over all day, but everything he thinks of is small and doesn't seem important. Pennies, buttons, beads, paper towels, rubber bands. Harry wants to bring something *big*. Something special.

At the end of the day, he puts on his coat. Then he gets his backpack. His Gar-Gar key chain swings back and forth jauntily.

Oh! He has an idea. "I'll bring one hundred Fluff Monsters!" he shouts as they are lining up.

"Harry, please use your indoor voice," says Ms. Peek-Schnitzel.

Mason grabs Harry's arm and jumps up and down, smiling. "Wow," he says. "That is the best thing to bring."

Harry bounces as he walks out to the yard for pickup. FLUFF MONSTERS!

DAY 89. MONDAY, JANUARY 28

"Are you really bringing one hundred Fluff Monsters?" Diamond asks Harry before morning meeting.

"Yep."

"How will you get them?"

"Buy them, I guess." Harry gets a sinking feeling in his tummy.

"They cost like five dollars each for the key chains," says Diamond. "That's what my mom says."

"Five dollars for one hundred monsters is . . . well, it's a lot of money, isn't it?" says Harry.

"Like, *a lot* a lot. Do you have *a lot* a lot of money?" Diamond asks hopefully.

No. Harry doesn't.

Then and there, Diamond loans Harry the three Fluff Monster key chains off her backpack. With those plus Harry's Gar-Gar, he has four Fluff Monsters. That's a good start.

"You still have to get to one hundred, though," says Diamond, sounding worried.

Oh, yeah. That's still *a lot* a lot.

But Harry can do it. And he has to, because he already told Ms. Peek-Schnitzel he was bringing Fluff Monsters. She even wrote it down on her clipboard.

He will go full Fluff.

DAY 90. TUESDAY, JANUARY 29

This morning, Ms. Peek-Schnitzel writes new words on the Sight Word Wall: *this, wish, know,* and *thank.*

Harry copies them down, but he isn't thinking about them.

He is thinking about getting ninety-six more Fluff Monsters.

The teacher asks them all to write short sentences using their new word-wall words.

Harry writes:

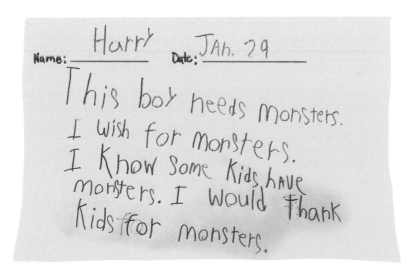

Name: Harry   Date: JAn. 29

This boy needs monsters.
I wish for monsters.
I know some kids have monsters. I would thank kids for monsters.

"Is it a poem?" asks Ms. Peek-Schnitzel, leaning over Harry's paper.

"No," he tells her. "It's my real life. Can I read it to everybody?"

She says yes. Harry stands up and reads his sentences aloud.

He hopes that other kids besides Diamond will help him out.

But what if they don't?

Chapter 18
KIMANI

DAY 91. WEDNESDAY, JANUARY 30

Kimani comes to school with three Fluff Monster toys and five key chains, some of which she borrowed from her brothers. She lends them to Harry.

Mason brings two Fluff Monster key chains and two puppets.

Abigail lends Harry four key chains.

Wyatt lends Harry his key chain. Robbie brings his. Amira brings hers. Mia brings two. Adam brings one. Maddie brings one. Elijah brings one.

And Ms. Peek-Schnitzel lends her two homemade puppets, the ones she used for the election. Twenty-five new monsters plus Harry's own and Diamond's three makes twenty-nine Fluff Monsters.

Harry shoves them all in his backpack. It is so fat and full that he can barely carry it home.

He is lucky to have such good friends. But he still needs seventy-one more.

DAY 92. THURSDAY, JANUARY 31

Today, Kimani is doing finger knitting with bright yellow yarn. She loops it around her finger and sort of braids it. It's getting very long. Diamond and Abigail want to know how. Kimani shows them.

"Do you guys want to know, too?" Kimani asks the boys at Goat Table.

"Nuh-uh," says Mason. "Yarn is dumb."

"Yeah, yarn is dumb," says Harry, just because Mason said it.

"Yarn is for girls," says Wyatt.

"Not true," says Kimani. "Yarn is for everybody. Everything is for everybody. Didn't your parents teach you that?"

At recess, Harry wants to play Sharks and Minnows. The kids from Goat Table have been playing it together at recess for the past couple of weeks. But today, Diamond and Abigail are cozied underneath the climbing structure with Kimani.

"It's time for Sharks and Minnows," Harry tells them, peeking under the structure.

"No thanks," says Abigail.

"We're finger knitting," says Diamond.

"Okay, then. Fine. We don't need you anyway," says Harry.

But three is not enough people for Sharks and Minnows.

Harry, Mason, and Wyatt try joining Elijah and Robbie, but those guys are busy with something called Goat and Unicorn.

They try joining Amira and Isabella, but those guys are busy with something called Tricky Pig Tricky Fox.

They stand with their backs against the brick wall. They don't know what else to do.

"Do you want to learn to finger knit?" asks Harry finally.

"No way," says Wyatt.

"No way," says Mason.

So they stand there, together, for the rest of recess.

DAY 93. FRIDAY, FEBRUARY 1

Abigail, Kimani, and Diamond are finger knitting at recess *again*. Kids are running all over, playing and shouting, but with no girls to play Sharks and Minnows, Harry, Wyatt, and Mason find themselves with their backs to the brick wall, just like yesterday.

It's cold outside. No one says anything.

"I miss the girls," Harry says finally.

"Me too," says Mason.

"Heh heh," says Wyatt.

"Don't say the kissing rhyme," warns Harry. "It's not that."

"I wasn't gonna," says Wyatt.

"I just want to play Sharks and Minnows with them," says Harry.

Wyatt frowns, thinking. "I miss the girls, too," he says. Then he asks, "What's the difference between boogers and broccoli?"

Harry doesn't know.

"They're both green?" guesses Mason.

"No," says Wyatt. "What's the *difference*?"

Harry thinks some more. "One is bigger," he guesses.

Wyatt shakes his head.

"What is it, then?" Harry asks.

"Kids don't eat broccoli," says Wyatt.

Ha! Harry and Mason fall over laughing. Eating boogers is so gross. And kind of true.

"I learned to tell a joke," says Wyatt.

DAY 94. MONDAY, FEBRUARY 4

Over the weekend, Harry thought about how to get seventy-one Fluff Monsters.

On Saturday, he couldn't figure out any way to get them.

On Sunday, he couldn't figure out any way to get them.

But today is Monday, and he knows a way! "Kimani, could I have some of your yarn?" he asks as they sit down to eat lunch.

"I have yarn, but you said it's dumb, so I think I'm going to keep it," says Kimani.

Oh. That wasn't as easy as Harry thought it would be.

During recess, Harry, Mason, and Wyatt climb to the top of the Rocket. They decide the top landing is a Boy Goat hideout, with no girls allowed. "We don't need girls, or yarn, or Sharks and Minnows," says Harry.

But that doesn't solve Harry's Fluff Monster problem.

DAY 95. TUESDAY, FEBRUARY 5

Harry has a plan to get yarn from Kimani. He finds Charlotte at recess, doing jump rope with Rosie and some other fourth-grade girls.

"Will you buy me some cheese puffs after school?" he asks.

"Say please," she tells him.

"Please and thank you very much," he says.

"Okay," she says, ruffling his hair.

"Your little brother is adorable," says one of the jumping girls.

Harry runs away.

DAY 96. WEDNESDAY, FEBRUARY 6

Harry gives Kimani his bag of cheese puffs at lunch. The whole bag that Charlotte bought for him.

"What's this for?" she asks, wrinkling her forehead.

"*I* want cheese puffs," says Mason. "I'm your best friend."

"I'm trading it for yarn," says Harry. "Could I have some yarn, please?"

"I don't know," says Kimani. "You act like it's so dumb, and now you want some?"

"It's not dumb," says Harry, but his voice comes out small.

"It's what?" asks Kimani.

"Yarn is not dumb," Harry says, loudly this time.

"Yarn is smart, and I would like some, please and thank you very much."

"Of course you can have some," says Kimani. "Yarn is for everybody."

During free time at the end of the day, Harry winds the yarn he got from Kimani tightly around a plastic fork. Then he ties it tight to make a bundle. He uses scissors to cut the looped ends of the yarn and fluffs it into round pom-poms, just like Kimani's mom taught them to do.

A little glue, two googly eyes from Ms. Peek-Schnitzel's supply cupboard, and . . . Harry has a home-made Fluff Monster.

One homemade, plus the twenty-nine he has at home, that's thirty.

Now he just needs seventy more to make one hundred.

Chapter 19
FLUFF MONSTERS

DAY 97. THURSDAY, FEBRUARY 7

The weather today is terrible. Freezing, freezing cold.

Harry is happy, though, because it means they stay indoors for recess.

And he has his own yarn now. Evaline took him to the craft-supply store in Manhattan after school and they bought two colors of fluffy yarn: red and purple. It cost only four dollars for both, plus seven for two packs of googly eyes.

Harry brings his yarn and packs of googly eyes to the auditorium, where the kids play during indoor recess. He's going to make as many Fluff Monsters as he possibly can.

He sits on the steps that lead to the stage and starts to work.

Select the yarn
and cut it.
Stretch the yarn
and wrap it.
Tie the yarn
and cut it.
Eyeball, eyeball . . .
Done.

He notices that Abigail has sat down next to him. She doesn't like all the noises of the crowded auditorium. Some kids are playing Uno. Others are doing Happy Llama Sad Llama. Some are playing Snakes and Ladders.

"Can I play with you?" asks Abigail.

She already knows how to make pom-poms. And it's easy to add googly eyes.

Abigail helps Harry till the end of recess. Together they make eleven Fluff Monsters.

He already has the twenty he and Charlotte made on Wednesday night and the eight he and Mommy made this morning. With this new eleven, plus the thirty from before, Harry has seventy fluff monsters.

Thirty to go.

DAY 98. FRIDAY, FEBRUARY 8

Harry is so good at making pom-pom Fluff Monsters! He made ten after school yesterday, all by himself. He is like, an expert at it.

Hey, that means he's an expert again. First a guinea pig expert, and now a monster-making expert.

Pretty boss.

He only needs twenty more monsters. And there's the whole weekend to do them. Easy peasy.

DAY 99. MONDAY, FEBRUARY 11

Monday was fine. Whatever. Math, reading, all the usual stuff. At the end of the day, Ms. Peek-Schnitzel reminded the kids, "Go home and get your one hundred items ready. Tomorrow is our celebration."

Oh, no!

Harry's stomach goes flurpy, because he *forgot* to make the last four Fluff Monsters. *Forgot!*

Here is what happened:

Friday evening, he made sixteen Fluff Monsters with Mommy and Charlotte. But with four more to go, they ran out of yarn.

No problem, though. That weekend, Harry and Charlotte were going to visit Daddy. "You can make them in Boston," said Mommy. "Your dad will know where to buy yarn, and I'll pack your googly eyes."

Early Saturday morning, Daddy picked up Harry and Charlotte and took them to Boston on the train. They went to a movie and out for burgers. The kids slept on Daddy's foldout couch.

On Sunday, they went to a children's museum, then to a place that served thirty kinds of pie. Late afternoon, Daddy took them on the train back to New York, and Mommy met them at Penn Station. She brought them back to Brooklyn, super tired, late at night.

Harry forgot to ask for yarn. In fact, he forgot about Fluff Monsters entirely for two whole days.

Now it's Monday, the one-hundredth day celebration is tomorrow, and Harry has only ninety-six Fluff Monsters—and no yarn! Even worse, he's not going home after school. He has a playdate with Mason. Evaline will pick him up after dinner.

"'Scuse me, Mason's dad?" Harry asks, in the schoolyard. "Do you maybe have yarn at your house I could use for a project? And forks and scissors and googly eyes?" asks Harry.

"Forks, scissors, and googly eyes, yes—but I don't think we have any yarn. Sorry, Harry."

"Could we go shopping for yarn? There's a craft store in Manahattan. Please and thank you very much."

Mason's dad is sorry, again, but no. Manhattan is far away and he has a lot of cooking to do, plus a work phone call from four to five.

"Could I call my mom, then?" asks Harry.

"Of course."

At Mason's apartment, Harry calls Mommy at work. "Will you buy yarn on your way home and we'll make Fluff Monsters tomorrow?" he asks.

"I don't get off until nine tonight," she says. "The stores won't be open. Maybe you and Mason can figure out how to make them some other way?"

"I guess," says Harry, but he is definitely worried.

Harry and Mason try. First, they build Fluff Monsters with Play-Doh.

"Hm," says Mason. "My monster is lumpy."

"Yeah," says Harry. "Mine is sticky."

"They look like potatoes," says Mason.

"Sticky blue potatoes," says Harry.

They try making Fluff Monsters out of crumpled origami paper instead. The monsters are fun to make, but the googly eyes won't stick to the crumples. "They just look like trash," says Harry, discouraged.

"Let's draw them with crayons," says Mason. "We're super good at them."

They draw two monsters each. They *are* both awesome at drawing Fluff Monsters. But the drawings are not full fluff.

"I don't want to bring crayon drawings," says Harry. "I want to bring monsters."

"Yeah," says Mason.

"I give up," says Harry.

"I give up, too," says Mason. "Even Pebble gives up."

They go into the kitchen and ask Mason's dad for a snack. He gives them pickles and baby carrots.

They take the food to the living room and sit on the floor in front of the coffee table. They are sad about the monsters, but they eat the pickles first and then dip the carrots in the pickle juice.

Suddenly Harry gets an idea. "Problem solved!" he cries. And he tells Mason his idea.

"Full fluff!" says Mason.

Together they run to the kitchen to talk to Mason's dad. "Can you help me text Diamond and Abigail?" Mason asks.

His dad says yes.

They text.

Ten minutes later, everything is great.

Harry is absolutely, totally, going full fluff.

DAY 100. TUESDAY, FEBRUARY 12

On the one-hundredth day of his first-grade year, Harry skips to school. He has two fabric tote bags full of Fluff Monsters, store-bought and homemade. Charlotte is carrying them so he can skip.

Fluff One Hundred!
That's full Fluff!

Fluff One Hundred!

That's full Fluff!

That is the song Harry skips to as he goes to school.

Though maybe it is a poem.

Or maybe it's a song *and* a poem.

Abigail, Mason, and Diamond are waiting outside the Graham School in their Halloween costumes.

Mason is dressed as Boompus, the purple Fluff Monster.

Diamond is Gorf, the green one.

Abigail is Dumpler, the red and orange one.

And Harry is Gar-Gar.

Twenty-seven store-bought monsters, two home-made puppets, sixty-seven pom-pom monsters, and four costumes makes one hundred.

The four Fluff Monsters go into Ms. Peek-Schnitzel's first-grade classroom. All the kids have brought their one hundred things.

Diamond has one hundred white toy jewels that are supposed to be diamonds.

Kimani has one hundred pink erasers, the kind that fit on the end of a pencil.

Mason did one hundred drawings of dogs on a poster board.

Wyatt has one hundred marshmallows, but they are only the miniature kind.

Abigail has one hundred pieces of dog kibble.

Ms. Peek-Schnitzel brought a jigsaw puzzle with one hundred pieces. She lays it out on one table. Kids can help put it together, if they want.

Wyatt comes up and pats Harry's monster suit. "It's so boss," he says. "Gar-Gar is my favorite."

"Do you want to wear it?" asks Harry. "You could be the one-hundredth fluff monster. It doesn't have to be me."

"For real?" says Wyatt.

"Sure," says Harry. "Be Gar-Gar."

"Cool, thanks!" says Wyatt. He puts on the Gar-Gar costume over his clothes. "Whomple whomple!" he yells, because that's the noise Fluff Monsters make when they run. The suit is a little short on him, but other than that, Wyatt really does make a good Gar-Gar.

After playtime is morning meeting. Diamond is Calendar right now, and she leads the song.

What is today? Tuesday, Tuesday.

What was yesterday? Monday, Monday.

What is tomorrow? Wednesday, Wednesday.

"And today is the one-hundredth day!" yells Diamond, when the song is over. She writes the number one hundred on their class calendar.

Everyone cheers.

Then Ms. Peek-Schnitzel gives out new jobs. And guess what? Harry gets to be Line Leader. At last, at last!

The kids all share what they brought for the one-hundredth day.

There are one hundred

diamonds

erasers

drawings of dogs

marshmallows

pieces of dog kibble

lipstick kisses on a poster board

Matchbox cars

sequins glued onto paper

tiny plastic animals

grains of rice

song titles listed on a printout

holes punched in paper

star stickers stuck on paper

bobby pins

nails

toothpicks

playing cards

dried beans

bottle caps

drinking straws

fingerprints on paper

pieces of pasta in different shapes

Pokémon cards

drawings of hearts

and

Fluff Monsters!

Harry shows his store-bought ones, the teacher's two puppets, his pom-pom ones, and his four friends. That makes one hundred.

Ms. Peek-Schnitzel gives each kid a bag with one hundred tiny snacks. Twenty-five cheese-flavored bunny crackers, twenty-five pretzel circles, twenty-five M&M's, and twenty-five Teddy Grahams. She also brought twenty-five small lemonades in cardboard boxes, so everyone gets a drink. Wyatt shares his one hundred mini marshmallows, and each kid gets four.

Mason, Diamond, and Abigail feel too hot in their costumes, so they take them off and just wear their regular clothes. But Wyatt keeps the Gar-Gar suit on.

Harry eats the heads off his Teddy Grahams and cheese bunnies.

So does Mason.

So do Wyatt, Abigail, Diamond, and Kimani, until everyone at Goat Table has a pile of headless treats. Then they eat the bodies and laugh.

The classroom is noisy but not too loud. Ms. Peek-

Schnitzel is talking about finishing up and heading to library soon, but nobody is paying attention.

Mason is trying to wiggle his not-wiggly tooth.

Abigail and Kimani are showing off their matching finger-knit friendship bracelets. Wyatt is telling his booger joke to Diamond.

Harry feels big. It's a special day. He grins his gappy smile. "You know what?" he says, going up to Ms. Peek-Schnitzel at her desk. "I got to be an expert three times already."

"You did?"

"Yes. I'm a guinea-pig expert. And a pom-pom-monster-making expert. And now I think I am a first-grade expert."

"You are? Tell me about it."

"Well, I could tell little kids all about first grade. I can explain it to them so they won't be scared."

"What would you tell them about first grade?" asks the teacher.

Harry thinks. "I'd say, don't push. Don't battle with

bead wires. Recycle. Use your words to say your feelings. Write your sight words. Practice counting to one hundred." He bites his lower lip and concentrates, wanting to remember everything important. "Don't eat the pumpkin snacks. Try to make new friends. Keep reading even when the words are hard. Speak up when something's wrong. And help when someone's sad."

"You did it!" cries Ms. Peek-Schnitzel. "You became an expert. Guinea pigs, monster making, *and* first grade. Fantastic!"

"Yup," says Harry.

And Harry Bergen-Murphy, first grader, thoughtful brother, reader of words with silent *E,* best friend to Mason, and now an expert three times over, skips off to get some lemonade.

Author's Note
For parents, teachers, librarians, and curious kids

Harry goes to a public school in Brooklyn, New York. With a little poetic license, I used the New York City Department of Education calendar to decide which days school would be closed and for what reasons. The story is set in the 2018–2019 school year, but I moved the dates of Hanukkah to suit my story better. I also used poetic license for the neighborhood, which is a composite of three in which I have lived, with street, business, and school names largely of my own invention.

As the school year progresses, Ms. Peek-Schnitzel's word walls will of course have many more words on them than are mentioned in the story. She puts up sight words every week, and sparkly words whenever they come up in reading or conversation. The ones below are only those specifically mentioned in the book.

Sight words

yes, no, me, you
friend, tired, play, happy
first, again, because, only
his, her, old, stop
this, wish, know, thank

Sparkly Word Wall

weird
usual
unusual
indigenous

election
gratitude
you're welcome
tradition
peaceful
reduce
reuse
recycle

Ms. Peek-Schnitzel asks the children to make family circles instead of the more conventional family trees. Classic family tree assignments can be stressful for students because they suggest that everyone's family is structured like a tree. Of course, that isn't so. Circles allow for all family configurations to be represented.

Fluff Monsters, for better and for worse, are imaginary. So are Harry's leveled-reader stories—the girl with the blob in the bowl and the mule who waves when she is baking. Spider-Man, My Little Pony, Harry Potter, and Captain Underpants are real, though—and very easy to find on video and in bookstores and libraries. So is the chapter book about the bear who might be named Edward. It is *Winnie-the-Pooh*.

What about the other stories referenced in *One Hundred Days*? They are all real picture books that I love sharing with children.

- The book about the boy and his grandmother on the bus is *Last Stop on Market Street* by Matt de la Peña, illustrated by Christian Robinson.

- The book about the boy in the wrestling costume is *Niño Wrestles the World* by Yuyi Morales.

- The book about wild boars is *Meet Wild Boars* by Meg Rosoff, illustrated by Sophie Blackall.

- Harry's imaginary-friend pillowcase costume idea is from *The Adventures of Beekle: The Unimaginary Friend* by Dan Santat.

- Diamond's moose costume idea is from *Z Is for Moose* by Kelly Bingham, illustrated by Paul O. Zelinsky.

- Abigail's costume idea is from *Sophie's Squash* by Pat Zietlow Miller, illustrated by Anne Wilsdorf.

- Ms. Peek-Schnitzel's costume comes from *Pug Meets Pig* by Sue Lowell Gallion, illustrated by Joyce Wan.

- The book the class reads for Election Day is *Grace for President* by Kelly DiPucchio, illustrated by LeUyen Pham.

- The book about the naked tiger is *Mr. Tiger Goes Wild* by Peter Brown.

- For Martin Luther King Day, the students read *Martin's Big Words* by Doreen Rappaport, illustrated by Bryan Collier.

- The book about the boy and the hungry snake in the eucalyptus tree is *One Day in the Eucalyptus, Eucalyptus Tree* by Daniel Bernstrom, illustrated by Brendan Wenzel.

- The Goat and Unicorn game comes from *Unicorn Thinks He's Pretty Great* by Bob Shea.

- The Tricky Pig, Tricky Fox game comes from *My Lucky Day* by Keiko Kasza.

As for guinea pigs, there are tons of educational videos online, but my favorite so far is by Little Adventures (maker of many guinea pig videos). This one has adorable creatures and a lot of information; plus, it's only two minutes long: youtube.com/watch?v=icEiRGp9cdQ.

The Cape Cod song is a classic sea chanty that I first heard on Dan Zanes's record *Sea Music;* it's a great recording and the singer is Father Goose, AKA Rankin Don. "Who Are the People in Your Neighborhood?" is a classic Sesame Street song, easy to find online. The Muppet community workers are all male in most iterations of the song, which dates the videos, but they're pretty great anyhow.

The llama rhyme in the book is the version my kid friends and I do in Brooklyn. There are a lot of different adaptations out there, though. Don't worry if yours is different.

The computer programs Ms. DeRosa uses are Keyboard Zoo at abcya.com and Bees and Honey at tvokids.com.

Making tiny pom-poms with yarn, scissors, and a fork is an easy project to do with some adult supervision. I recommend this tutorial by Giddyup Workshop: youtube.com/watch?v=fjxJFcm16r0.

Happy first one hundred days of school!

Gratitude

I am grateful for help with this book. Thanks to my editor, Anne Schwartz, for all her hard work with this very tricky structure; and to my agent, Elizabeth Kaplan; and to the greatly skilled people at Random House who have supported my books for more than thirteen years. Sarah Mlynowski critiqued a draft. Bob was always there for me. Kate Messner and Anne Ursu helped with contacts. Stella Bourne, Ivy Aukin, and Hazel Aukin gave me many helpful suggestions, and Hazel shared her best booger jokes. Freshly graduated from first grade, Elise Bogaty shared her knowledge. Daniel Aukin was awesome.

Rosemary Wells's funny and sensitive long-form picture book *Emily's First 100 Days of School* was an inspiration for this project.

In my late teens and twenties, I worked as an assistant in a number of preschools. I also spent a year assistant-teaching in an ages-six-to-nine classroom at a Montessori school. Still, I needed significant input from experienced educators to shape the activities at the Graham School. Second-grade teacher Chris Black and first-grade teacher Rebecca Austern offered many social-, emotional-, and curriculum-related insights. Melissa Kantor and Heather Weston connected me to them. Linda Coombs lent her expertise. I'm also indebted to the websites of teachers and reading specialists who share their ideas and practices, including but not limited to *Miss Giraffe's Class, The Brown Bag Teacher, Mrs. Brown Art, Literacy and Lattes, What I Learned Teaching,* and *Mrs. Beattie's Classroom.*